# the labyrinth campaign

### a novel

## j. michael sweeney

LIVE OAK
BOOK COMPANY

Published by Live Oak Book Company
Austin, Texas
www.liveoakbookcompany.com

Distributed by Live Oak Book Company

For ordering information or special discounts for bulk purchases, please contact Live Oak Book Company at PO Box 91869, Austin, TX 78709, 512.891.6100.

Design and composition by Greenleaf Book Group LLC
Cover design by Tom Nynas, RUCKER & CO., Dallas, TX

Publisher's Cataloging-In-Publication Data
(Prepared by The Donohue Group, Inc.)
Sweeney, J. Michael (John Michael), 1961-
    The labyrinth campaign : a novel/ J. Michael Sweeney. — 1st ed.
    p. ; cm.
    Issued also as an ebook.
    Includes bibliographical references.
    ISBN: 978-1-936909-28-5
    1. Businessmen—United States—Fiction. 2. Presidents—United States—Election—Fiction. 3. Presidential candidates—United States—Fiction. 4. Conspiracy—United States—Fiction. 5. Texas—Fiction. 6. Political fiction. I. Title.
PS3619.W44 L23 2011
813/.6                                                    2011940923

Print ISBN: 978-1-936909-28- 5
eBook ISBN: 978-1-936909-29-2

First Edition

# Acknowledgments

To my wife, Pat: Without her this book would never have happened.

To Jack, Janci, and Spencer: Thanks for being who you are and keeping me on my toes.

To Jacque, Rosanne, Catherine, and Doug: Thanks for helping me get this thing done.

To the rest of my family, friends, and colleagues: Thanks for being part of what makes life meaningful.

To everyone else: Be kind, be gracious, be peaceful.

# A Note to the Reader

The contents and characters in this book are purely fiction. The journey of creating The Labyrinth Campaign began in 1997, long before our most recent president from Texas announced his intentions to run for office and also well before the events of 9/11 forever changed our view of terrorism as tragedies that happened "somewhere else."

If any of the characters or events in this novel are offensive to you, please accept my sincere apology. The intention of this book was to create a suspenseful plot that allowed a moment of "suspended belief," not a story that reminded us of our current reality.

Hope you enjoy.

# one

It was evening in London, a time when the city should have been filled with the masses of humanity who had gotten off of work a few hours earlier. But the streets were nearly deserted. The driving rain that had continued throughout the day had either sent the Londoners home for the evening or into one of the local pubs where they could dry off with a nice pint. But on St. Martens Lane, two young men seemed oblivious to the persistent downpour. Walking with purpose, Don Juan and Billy the Kid—as their Oxford schoolmates called them—were looking for their next stop on a daylong pub crawl. It wasn't that they actually needed more to drink, but it was their last night in London before returning home after graduation from university. They were on a mission to find The Standard, an establishment highly recommended by Keith, the bartender at their last stop. As the two rounded the corner near Trafalgar Square, they spotted the pub across the street. Last chance to meet some girls before the night got away from them.

When they opened the front door, the sounds and smells of the densely packed bar greeted them. They looked at each other happily and entered. The Standard was a typical London pub. The smoke-filled air, dark mahogany bar to the right, and tables and chairs against the wall to the left made this place feel like every other pub they had been to. The only difference was the crowd. The two young men headed straight for the far end of the bar, set on ordering quickly and efficiently. When they got there, they saw two stools that had just been vacated. They settled in, determined to make their last night in London a memorable one.

Typical for two young men who had just graduated from university, their conversation volleyed between girls and career aspirations. As the career discussion evolved, the American turned to his Mexican friend and said, "I don't know why I sit here and speculate about my career options. My dad already has it all planned out: a couple of years networking in the Texas oil business just to get the right contacts, then straight into politics. I've already been told in no uncertain terms that I will be the president of the United States."

"Well," the young Mexican responded, "you never know when knowing the president of the United States might come in handy." They both laughed.

As the discussion continued, the young man from Mexico City outlined his own career direction. He explained, "My father has not determined such a defined career track for me, but he is a structured man and expects me to have goals, and I have one. I will one day be the richest man in Mexico, and I'll do whatever it takes to get there. Starting tomorrow." They both laughed again.

"The crazy thing is," the American said, "my family is viewed as one of the most influential, upstanding families in our entire country. What a crock of shit. Our wealth and power have come at the conscious expense of others. My father has lied, cheated, coerced, blackmailed, and philandered to get his way. He is truly Machiavellian; in his mind, the end does justify the means." The young American shook his head, took a long pull at his pint, then continued. "It's funny; while I'm fully aware of my father's shortcomings, I'm somehow driven to be just like him. The only difference is that he is hell-bent on insulating me from the family's underhanded dealings so I can one day be the most powerful man in the world."

The young Mexican aristocrat nodded in understanding. "My family truly was the most influential, upstanding family in all of Mexico. Our financial and political influence was unprecedented. But when you wield that much power, there is always someone gunning for you. Unfortunately, in my father's case, it was the brother of our current president." The young man paused as he took a big swig of ale. "Slowly, but surely, this jealous, untalented, but well-connected man chipped away at our family's business. A condemned warehouse here, a denied radio-license renewal there, coupled with the insatiable spending habits of my father, and the next thing you know, we're strapped for cash."

A crash behind the two young men interrupted their conversation as they turned to see two young Brits standing toe to toe, slugging it out. They watched as a brawny bartender casually stepped in to break up the fight, then turned back to their pints.

"So, all of a sudden my family is right in the middle of a significant financial crisis," the young Mexican continued. "My father soon realized he was not going to weather the storm on his own, so he turned to a friend from his hometown of Saltillo. His old friend, however, had made his fortune trafficking drugs. The deal was simple. If my father provided use of his legitimate trucking company for moving drugs to northern Mexico storage facilities, his friend would provide the cash infusion necessary to restore my family's wealth." The young Mexican sighed, "So my family is back on its feet, but when I return to Mexico City, I will inherit a diverse, thriving conglomerate with a significant drug business as its foundation." The two silently sipped their pints, each of them pondering the future.

Staring into his glass, the young American felt the buzz between his eyes intensifying. The thick, dark English beer they had been drinking really packed a punch. At that moment, a female voice asked, "Is this stool taken?" He looked around, realizing his friend must have gone to the loo. As he looked up at the girl to tell her it was taken, he was face-to-face with the prettiest girl he had seen in England. And her friend looked pretty good, too.

He immediately stood and said, "We would be more than happy to give up our seats for two beautiful girls such as yourselves. That is, if you don't mind two average Joes like us standing nearby trying to figure out how to talk to you."

The girls laughed, and the first one said, "You're more than welcome to stay, but your invisible friend seems rather the bore."

It was then that he realized they hadn't seen his Mexican friend. "Oh, I'm here with a buddy. I'm sure he'll be right back."

As if on cue, his companion returned. "Bueno, bueno, my good friend," he said, smiling. "You have been busy while I've been gone." As he extended his hand to introduce himself, he quickly scanned two of the most attractive girls he'd seen since he'd been in England. This night was turning out to have all the potential that seemed lost just a few short minutes ago.

As the four new acquaintances exchanged small talk, the two young men failed to notice a couple of British military types come in the front door. As the new arrivals stepped up to the bar and ordered, one of the men with hair cropped unstylishly short gave his companion a sideways nod, gesturing toward the two girls. The girls had not noticed them, however, and seemed to hang on every word from the recent Oxford graduates. This went on for nearly twenty minutes until finally, the two observers had had enough. They approached the four, who were laughing at some joke. One of the girls looked up and said, "There you two are! We've been wondering where you've been."

The older of the two soldiers said, "Really? We've been watching you for nearly half an hour and didn't notice you look to the door even once." The two girls looked shocked and a little uneasy. The soldiers looked angry, not at the girls, but at the intruders. The graduates knew it was time to make a graceful exit or have a messy confrontation on their hands.

The young American made the first move. "Well, now that your friends are here, I guess we'll be going."

The stockier of the two soldiers said, "No, wait; we were interested in what was so funny when we walked up."

"I honestly don't remember; it must have been nothing."

"Nothing?" the younger soldier said. "Two asshole foreigners hitting on our girlfriends, I don't call that nothing."

With that, the young Mexican stood; he was a pretty good-sized man but didn't have nearly the athletic physique of his American friend. He said, "Hey, we didn't know they were your girlfriends, nor were we hitting on them, so fuck off. We said we were leaving."

The two young men quickly said their goodbyes and headed for the side exit. When they entered the alley outside of the bar, they were both angry, not only at the confrontation, but also at the prospect of going home alone—again.

Just then, the door opened behind them, and the two soldiers stepped into the dank, dark alley. The older soldier snarled, "Did we tell you two you were dismissed?"

"Dismissed?" the young Mexican yelled, his fists balling up. "We don't need your permission for shit."

The American stepped forward. "Hey, we don't want any trouble, and we said we were leaving."

The stockier soldier responded, "Well, you got trouble," and hit the young American in the face with the force of an experienced heavyweight. Surprisingly, the American did not go down; he stood there shocked and silent for what seemed an eternity. Then, like a predator, he pounced. The surprise of suddenly not having the upper hand slowed the soldier's response. In an instant, he was down with the American on top of him. At the same time, the Mexican and the younger soldier leapt at each other with a force that toppled them both to the ground.

The American was easily winning his end of the confrontation. The element of surprise, coupled with his raw athletic ability, had him on top of the older soldier repeatedly driving his fist into the already bloodied face. He struck again and again until he realized his foe was unconscious.

In an instant he was up looking to help his friend, who was not faring as well as he had. The Mexican was curled up in a fetal position, covering his head as best he could, while the young soldier stood over him, kicking him mercilessly. The American quickly looked around and picked a large piece of wood, broken off of an old crate, and took a full baseball swing at the head of the assailant. The soldier fell to the alley, and the enraged American struck him again and again.

The Mexican yelled, "Stop, you're going to kill him!"

The American stopped and gazed down at the motionless soldier. The adrenaline rush he felt at that moment told him that he would never again hesitate to do whatever it took to achieve his objectives.

# two

It was Indian summer in Boulder, Colorado. The warm September sun was shining down on the University of Colorado faithful who were hoping to see their Buffaloes win for the second time in as many weeks at Folsom Field, undoubtedly one of the most scenic college stadiums in the country. The Buffs had just scored the go-ahead touchdown with less than three minutes left in the game. If the defense could just hang on, the half-filled stadium would go nuts as the formidable University of Wisconsin Badgers were sent packing back to Madison.

It was third down and ten yards to go, and the ball was on Wisconsin's thirty-nine. The Badger quarterback took the snap and dropped back to pass as his tight end ran a delay from the right. He was wide open over the middle for what appeared to be an easy first down. A couple more of these and the Badgers would be in position to kick the winning field goal. The Wisconsin quarterback, under pressure, released the pass. The crowd was silent. From the booth, radio announcer Larry Zimmer had already counted first down in his own mind. Then, out of nowhere, junior linebacker Jack McCarthy streaked in front of the pass, diving for the game-clinching interception. When he snagged the ball, the crowd went crazy. The Buffs ran out the clock and won 21–19. News in all of Colorado, and big news in the small college town of Boulder.

Later that evening, as Jack drove down College Avenue in his turquoise 1976 Datsun B-210, he and his girlfriend, Shea Bennet, relived the afternoon's excitement. Since he had left the locker room, all of Jack's activities had included consumption of beer. First, he went to the Harvest House beer garden, where he and 3,000 of his closest friends celebrated CU's big win. Then, at home, he and his roommates sat around the kitchen table playing their favorite drinking game, Liar's Dice. Then after a quick shower, he was off to pick up Shea so they could hit his Delta Phi fraternity party on The Hill. As they expected, when they pulled up near the Delta Phi house, the party was already rocking.

As Shea and Jack fought their way to the front door, the crowd started to chant, "Jack, Jack, Jack, Jack." He was the celebrity for the evening. Before they even got to the front staircase, Jack and Shea were chugging beers, hugging drunken fraternity brothers, and smoking a joint of some of the best Thai stick they'd had in a while. Jack was enjoying the attention, but he was feeling the need for a breather from the crowd and the nearly forced beer consumption.

Just then, Charlie Hall, one of Jack's best friends from high school, grabbed Jack in a headlock and yelled, "Noogie!" as he viciously rubbed Jack's head.

Jack pushed Charlie away but then, when he realized who it was, said, "You asshole, are you ever going to grow up?"

"I hope not," Charlie responded. "Let's go upstairs, I've got some great blow."

"Oh, that's a shock," Jack retorted. "Let me get Shea, and I'll meet you in your room."

Twenty minutes later, after each had had three rails (a term Charlie claimed he invented), Jack said, "Hey, let's go back to the party."

"What are you talking about? We're just getting started," Charlie mumbled through coke-numbed lips.

"Don't you ever get enough?" Jack said. "I'm already flying."

"You sure are a pussy for such a big stud football player, Jack."

"Fuck you, Charlie. You're nothing more than a second-rate frat boy with a first-rate drug problem."

"I'm okay 'til you get your buzz, and then I'm a fuck-up, is that it?" Charlie fired back. Then, without warning, he threw a beer bottle that caught Jack right in the chest. Without hesitation, Jack threw Charlie to the ground and pulled back his right fist, ready to pummel Charlie's face.

Shea grabbed Jack's arm and screamed, "What the hell are you guys doing? I thought you were friends!" Then she spun on her heel and said, "I'm outta here."

Jack and Charlie stared at each other silently. Then they both started to laugh. Charlie said, "Sorry about the bottle, man."

"Yeah, I'm sorry about what I said, too. I'm just worried about you. You're doing too much shit."

"Don't worry about me, man. I got it under control."

"I hope so, dude, but I gotta catch Shea. She's pissed."

"Go ahead," Charlie said as Jack raced from the room. "I'll call you tomorrow."

As Jack caught Shea at the front door of the frat house, she yanked her arm away. "Shea, I'm sorry. I don't know what got into me. Actually, that's not true, I do know what got into me: that goddamned cocaine."

"You always want more, and it makes you do some crazy things."

"Shea, I swear to you, I'll never do that shit again. It screws up people's lives."

"I agree. I won't do it anymore if you won't."

They silently embraced on the front steps of the Delta Phi house, smiled at each other, and walked toward the car hand in hand as the chants of "Jack, Jack, Jack," echoed down the tree-lined residential street.

As Jack and Shea drove back to his house, Jack observed, "I can name five guys in our house who are doing too much coke. The stuff is so easy to get, these guys are doing it every day. Now Charlie is getting an ounce at a time, dealing enough to pay the tab, and snorting the rest."

"Jack, you can't live their lives for them; all you can do is tell your real friends how you feel."

"I know, but what's this world coming to? Drugs on every street corner in every neighborhood in America, air pollution choking the environment. The people of the world better wake up soon, or we're all fucked."

"Wow, Jack, you are getting old," Shea said. "You were the star of the game this afternoon, and tonight, instead of reliving that play a hundred and fifty times like you would have last year, you're discussing the world's problems."

Jack looked at her and grinned.

Later, as Jack and Shea lay in bed, Jack realized he still had serious thoughts running through his mind. Drugs . . . nuclear threats. "I can't believe I've been so stupid, Shea. I've done coke lots of times, when I know it has the potential to kill me at any moment."

"Jack, everyone is doing it, and I haven't heard of anyone dying in Boulder from too much coke."

"That's not the point, Shea. All it takes is one person, even an athlete with a heart problem, and bam! The heart explodes. And you know what that means."

"Yeah, it means you're being overly dramatic," Shea said. They both laughed.

"But seriously, Shea—"

"Hey, Jack. Can we stop saving the world and go to sleep? Or better yet, fool around?"

"Now that's an issue we can both agree on."

She giggled and turned out the light.

The next morning, as they lay asleep in each other's arms, Jack's bedside phone rang. He sleepily fumbled to pick up the receiver. "Hello."

"Jack, it's Dave." Dave was Charlie's roommate at the Delta Phi house.

"No, Dave, I can't pick you guys up for breakfast; I've got plans," Jack said as he stroked Shea's long, brown hair.

"That's not why I'm calling, man. I've got some bad news. Charlie died last night, Jack."

Jack bolted upright in bed as if he'd been touched by a hot cattle prod.

"He overdosed on cocaine, Jack. We found him this morning. I'm sorry to be the one to tell you. I know how close you two were."

Jack silently hung up the phone, and his head fell into his hands. He was too stunned to cry. But his course was set, he realized. The thoughts he had the night before suddenly crystallized into a hardened resolve: Drugs and the people who dealt them were the enemy that would bring this country to its knees.

Then the grief came: heavy sobs from deep down in his belly.

"God, Charlie, I miss you already."

# three

*[Twenty years later]*

The two men squared off, ready for battle, the student and the instructor. This particular student provided a rare challenge for the aging Tae Kwon Do instructor. As the two sparred, it was apparent that the student had keenly developed his skills. Quick, well-placed blows to his face and body quickly had the instructor retreating. The crowd of students seated around the ring watched in awe and envy as Jack McCarthy continued his relentless pursuit of the martial arts instructor who had pummeled him so many times. Following an exchange of blows that Jack had clearly won, the instructor raised both arms in the air, signaling the end of the match. Jack was elated. He'd never had so much success against such a worthy opponent.

As the instructor gathered the class for his final words of wisdom before dismissing them, he said, "I have a special announcement today. Jack McCarthy is ready for the next step. I am hereby awarding him a black belt."

Jack was stunned by the announcement. The rest of the class erupted in a loud cacophony of applause and screams. Jack, however, was silent. He never had any intention of being a black belt. He began his martial arts training to stay in shape; his knees were too battered from football to continue a heavy schedule of running, and a friend at work had turned him on to the mental and physical attributes of martial arts. This was truly a special moment for him.

After a long receiving line of handshakes and hugs from his fellow students, Jack hit the locker room for a shower and a shave before he called his girlfriend, Carrie, to invite her out for a celebration. When he finally left the martial arts studio, he stepped out into the evening air. The wall of heat hit him, reminding him that September is still summer in Dallas, Texas. As Jack drove down Greenville Avenue, his mind wandered from black belt to girlfriend to work and finally back to that warm feeling of accomplishment.

It was Friday night. Though it was still early, the bars and restaurants along Greenville Avenue were already filling up. This part of Lower Greenville was an interesting section of town. The gingerbread houses of the "M" streets were the location of choice for Dallas's young professionals. Close to downtown and within walking distance of a number of trendy bars and restaurants, the neighborhood was an ideal location. Jack was now older than the average M-street inhabitant, but he loved his house on Mercedes Street and continued to tell himself there was no reason to move until he got married. His office had always been downtown, and he could get there in less than fifteen minutes. His favorite restaurant was The Grape, and he could get there in less than five. What was not to like?

As Jack pulled his two-year-old Saab convertible into the driveway, his cell phone rang. "Hi," cooed Carrie, his new and very sexy girlfriend.

"Hey," Jack said. "Come over right now; we have some celebrating to do."

"Really? What's the occasion?"

"I just got my black belt, and I want to take you out for dinner."

"Oooh, sounds great. I can be there in about an hour. I just need to stop home and change real quick."

"Are you still at the office?" Jack asked.

"Yeah, check your voicemail and you'll know why. See you in a bit."

Jack wandered into his house, thinking about Carrie. She was awesome. Beautiful, smart, fun. If she only liked sports more, she would be perfect! But then again, no one was perfect.

Jack had four voicemail messages. The first was from Ross: tee time at 8:00 a.m., Saturday morning.

"Yes!" Jack hadn't played golf in weeks.

The next two messages were uneventful, but the final message explained what Carrie was talking about. It was from Allen Hamilton, the CEO of Will, Page, and Clark, the advertising agency where Jack and Carrie worked. WPC had just been notified that they had made it to the final round of the GenSquare new-business pitch, and Allen was calling an 8:00 meeting for Saturday morning. GenSquare, a next-generation software company, was the fastest growing company in Texas, owned by the Hawkins family, the richest and most powerful in the state.

Jack reacted with mixed emotions. The pitch was the biggest in the agency's history, but as silly as it sounded, he was really looking forward to playing golf. Anyway, business came first, not to mention the added bonus that William, the eldest son of the Hawkins family, was a powerful Texas senator with presidential aspirations. This would not normally be of much interest to Jack, but the senator and Jack had very similar views on Jack's two most passionate political topics: drugs and the environment.

Jack made a quick call to Ross to bail on golf and jumped into the shower. After getting dressed, he was startled by a noise in the kitchen. As he rounded the corner to investigate, he bumped squarely into Carrie. She was dressed impeccably, and the sight of her took his breath away.

"You look great! And I'm suddenly looking a little underdressed," he stated as he looked down at his jeans, starched, button-down shirt, and loafers.

"You look fine," Carrie replied. "I just got a little carried away, thinking about my black-belt boyfriend."

With that, she threw her arms around Jack and gave him a long, passionate kiss. Just as Jack began to respond, she pulled away and said, "Oh, no you don't! We've got dinner plans."

Jack feigned disappointment, grabbed his keys, and said, "Let's go. We're already looking at an hour wait at this time on a Friday night."

As the couple drove down Mercedes Street with the top down, the warm wind blowing through their hair, Carrie asked, "Did you get Allen's voicemail?"

"Yeah, can you believe we made the finals?"

The instant he said it, he wished he could take it back. Carrie was the new-business director at WPC, and his comment, while just intended as conversation, probably hit her like a slap in the face. "Hey," Jack said, "that didn't sound like I meant it to. You're the best new-business person in town, and I actually would have been shocked if we hadn't made it to the finals."

Carrie smiled and stroked Jack's hair. "Thanks, I needed that."

As Jack and Carrie drove down Greenville Avenue heading for The Grape, traffic began to slow. Lines were already out the door at many of the restaurants and bars.

As Jack wheeled into the valet alley at The Grape, Jeff, the regular attendant, called out, "Jack! Haven't seen you in a while."

Jeff opened the door for Carrie, walked to the front of the car, and high-fived the parking stub into Jack's hand.

The couple entered the restaurant. It was like stepping into a bistro in Paris: wine bar on the right, small, intimate dining room on the left. Mark, the manager, greeted Jack with a hearty handshake and Carrie with a hug.

Mark said, "I'll do my best, but it's probably going to be a half an hour."

"No problem, man," Jack responded. "We'll be at the bar."

They found two seats at the end of the five-seat bar and settled in. When their drinks came, Carrie proposed a toast. "To the night of the black belt."

Jack responded with, "To winning GenSquare."

They both smiled and drank. When Mark wandered by, Jack told him that they had decided to eat at the bar. After they ordered, a discussion regarding GenSquare began.

"If we win the account, Allen is going to assign you as managing partner," Carrie said.

"I know. And normally I'd view a new account of this size the same way I'd view a prison sentence. But this one's different," Jack confided. "First of all, I think their vision for a new software delivery system is brilliant. And, while I'm not overly political, the opportunity to work with the Hawkins family and the chance to meet Senator Will Hawkins is intriguing."

"Really? What's so intriguing about a rich, playboy, third-generation Democrat who bought his way into the Senate?"

Jack laughed. "Boy, aren't our Republican feathers ruffled!"

"No, really, Jack. What's so intriguing about Will Hawkins?"

Jack launched into a five-minute monologue. He told Carrie in detail about the night in college when he lost his best friend, Charlie, and told her how on that fateful night, his views on drugs and all things environmental were forever established. Carrie had never seen passion like this from Jack. But at that moment, she felt connected to him. In fact, she realized she was in love with him.

When they went back to Jack's place that evening, they made passionate love. They had celebrated their successes together; they had shared intimate details of their lives with each other, and their feelings for each other were cemented. They knew this relationship was something very deep and very special.

# four

The next morning Jack and Carrie drove into the office together. Though they hadn't gotten much sleep, they were energized by the feelings that had grown between them last night, as well as the challenge of the GenSquare pitch ahead of them. As they pulled into the parking lot of the opulent building that housed WPC corporate headquarters, it felt like any other workday. But it was Saturday, and there were few cars in the parking lot.

On rare occasions like this, Jack felt amazed that he had made it this far in the world of advertising. It hadn't been his career choice until his senior year of college. Prior to that, he had majored in football, beer, and girls—not necessarily in that order. Now he was on the team that would be pitching the single largest account in Texas advertising history. And if they won, he'd be running the account.

As the elevator doors opened, Carrie and Jack entered the posh lobby of WPC. Hardwood floors, a magnificent reception desk, leather furniture, and a wall of creative awards communicated that WPC was a force in the world of advertising. When they entered the boardroom at 8:10, the rest of the new-business team was already assembled.

"Glad you two decided you could make it," Allen Hamilton, the CEO, remarked.

"Sorry we're late," Jack responded, immediately knowing he'd just stuck his foot in his mouth. By implying that he and Carrie had arrived together, all previous efforts to hide their relationship had just been nullified. Carrie let out a nervous laugh as they took their seats at opposite ends of the massive boardroom table.

Allen spoke authoritatively. "Let's get started. As you all know, it's down to us and the Daniels Group for the biggest win in our agency's history. I want this account more than anything I've ever wanted in my life. Each of you must understand that the next few weeks are going to be grueling. This room will be our war room; we're going to live here. We will spare no expense. We are going to win the GenSquare Software account."

As Hamilton, the youngest agency president in Dallas history, gazed around the room, the best and brightest his agency had to offer were nodding in affirmation: Cindy Noble, chief creative officer, with twenty years of experience on Madison Avenue; Scott Parks, senior vice president for strategic planning—and company clown; Sharon Campbell, senior vice president of digital marketing and media; and Carrie and Jack. This was the team he had assembled to take on the monumental task of landing the GenSquare account.

Hamilton continued, "Not only is GenSquare the biggest opportunity in WPC history, but who knows what other doors a win with the Hawkins family might open." With that, Allen began the new-business briefing. GenSquare was the next generation of computer software, he told them. A customer would not actually purchase a software application and install it on a computer, nor would a company purchase multiple copies of a specific software application and install it on multiple machines in the same organization. Instead, GenSquare Software had identified an entirely new delivery system using existing network technology.

"Beginning next month, with significant Wall Street fanfare and capital, GenSquare will begin delivery of both proprietary and existing software to customers using previously installed broadband cable systems," Hamilton said. "Customers will pay a monthly access fee as well as usage charges. This has analysts predicting a revolution in the software industry.

"That, ladies and gentlemen, is the concept in a nutshell. We've been waiting for a new-business opportunity like this for ten years. And I'll be damned—no, let me rephrase that—we'll be damned if we're going to let this big fucking fish off the hook. Any questions?"

As the intensity of the moment settled in, no one said a word.

"Hey, don't go quiet on me now," Hamilton said. "This is the chance we've wanted for years. Reel this one in, and our futures and the future of our organization are set. You guys get what this means, right?"

As if a winning goal had just been scored, the room erupted in a loud exchange of yells, whistles, and high fives. When the noise subsided, Allen asked again, "So now, are there any questions?"

For the next ninety minutes the group discussed the strategic possibilities offered by such a distinct point of difference in the software industry. The conceptual juices that were flowing this Saturday morning would be the envy of any other advertising agency in America, Hamilton thought as he watched his team work. He had once again proven why WPC, under his guidance, had become one of the most successful agency resources in the US. He smiled to himself as he watched this talented group feed off each other and generate idea after idea.

Jack McCarthy hadn't felt this type of adrenaline rush since college football—the chance to impact the marketing world on a global scale, and the chance to work with the family of the front-runner for the next presidency of the United States.

# five

The Hawkins family mansion in the upscale Dallas neighborhood of Highland Park was one of the most opulent compounds in all of Texas. The main house was over 35,000 square feet, with a pool and guesthouse that added another 7,000 square feet. The main house fronted Beverly Drive, one of the most desired residential streets in the city. With a formal dining room that seated thirty-six, a kitchen that rivaled most fine restaurants, and a parlor that was larger than the average American home, the Hawkins estate was designed and built for high-class entertaining.

On this Saturday evening, however, there were no parties. In the family library—its collection the envy of many small colleges—Sen. William S. "Will" Hawkins and his father, William "Bo" Hawkins, were discussing the initial stages of Will's announcement of his intention to seek the Democratic nomination for president of the United States.

Some pundits thought the family's political affiliation odd, since most Texans with the wealth and stature of the Hawkins family were prominent, active members of the Republican Party. But not Bo and his family. He considered the Hawkins clan "true Texans" who had been loyal Democrats since long before the reign of Lyndon B. Johnson.

"Will, it's time to identify the key players who will help us get you elected," Bo Hawkins said to his son. "I'm dead set on John Rollins as your chief of staff. He's been our lead banker for twenty-five years, and he's extremely loyal to the family."

"What about Metroplex Bank? Will they release him from the presidency?"

"I'm sure the board of directors would be happy to let him go if we promise our account loyalty in his absence. We are the single largest account Metroplex has, after all. I also think it's time to find our key strategist."

Will cringed at the way his father continuously talked about his campaign with words like "we," "our," and "us," but his father's strength and imposing presence precluded him from speaking his mind—as they had for as long as Will could remember.

"Dad, Pete Robinson is my chief strategist. We've been friends since our undergrad days at college, and I know I can trust him."

"Pete's great, and we'll retain him, but he's been in politics his entire career," Bo said. "We need a marketer, someone who understands the motivations and mind-set of voters. Someone who treats you like a product, and voters like consumers."

Will kept his thoughts to himself. They ultimately agreed that Pete Robinson would work hand in hand with the yet-to-be-identified "consumer expert" as costrategists on the Hawkins campaign. Will and his father would begin the search immediately.

As father and son continued their conversation, the discussion shifted from presidential campaign to family business.

"Will, the volatility of the oil business has aged me beyond my years. If our oil holdings had been invested in other vehicles, we'd be worth twice what we are today." Bo stared out one of the library's floor-to-ceiling windows for a few seconds. "Real estate is a necessary part of any portfolio, but I've always believed that once your net worth surpasses $100 million, it should not account for more than 30 percent of your holdings. The stock market has been very good to us in the past ten years, but I hate to put someone else in control of my money. So that leads us to GenSquare.

"Will, GenSquare is my legacy to the Hawkins holdings and our family's future. We're having final presentations from our advertising agency finalists this week. I think it would be a good idea for you to sit in. The more you know about the guts of the family business, the better it'll be when you take over after your presidency."

They looked at each other and smiled.

# six

David Ellis sat in his Century City office gazing out at the panoramic view of the Hollywood Hills, Beverly Hills, and downtown Los Angeles. Ellis's meteoric rise from "cause-of-the-week" lawyer to the leader of the most powerful political organization outside the two major parties had surprised even him. The Future State Foundation was only three years old, and its endorsement was already considered a necessity when seeking public office. Senators, congressmen, and presidential hopefuls were already calling, hoping for endorsement from David and the foundation in next year's election.

The foundation was a unique liberal organization. Its focus was on the need for economic evolution, elimination of national debt, enhancement of the Social Security system, and, most importantly in Ellis's mind and those of his members, the need for an ecological revolution. Ellis contended that ecological dangers had never been greater. Nuclear proliferation and the corresponding waste due to expansion in the Middle East, North Korea, and China were a reality. Industrial pollution was increasing due to reductions in government oversight, especially in developing nations. "Dirty" power development was on the rise because power companies remained too profit-conscious to invest in alternative power research and development, and government engineers were just too bureaucratic to try anything new or controversial.

David Ellis and his Future State Foundation were capitalizing on these circumstances. The organization, with its highly efficient infrastructure, was recruiting new members at a staggering rate. Within months, the foundation membership would exceed the numbers generated by the NRA and the Christian Coalition combined.

Ellis was quickly becoming quite the celebrity. His emotionally charged speeches warning of the apocalyptic consequences associated with ignoring our economy and environment were universally admired. Many believed the US had not seen oratory skills of this magnitude since the 1960s with John F. Kennedy and Martin Luther King. David Ellis was on the "mountain top" and, while publicly disdainful of the attention, was actually quite enjoying it. First-class air travel, five-star hotels, press attention that politicians would die for, and women throwing themselves at him like he was a rock star. Yes, he was enjoying himself and doing it all on his own terms.

A knock on the door yanked David from his daydream. Skip Richards, his best friend, right-hand man, and confidant, was standing in the doorway.

Skip asked, "Did I interrupt your next revelation?"

"As a matter of fact, you did. I was just contemplating the therapeutic powers of the high life our newfound success has provided." Both laughed.

"David, it looks like Will Hawkins is going to run for the Democratic nomination."

"Yeah, not that we haven't been expecting it."

"Do you think he'll call?"

"No doubt in my mind," David quickly responded.

"But the Hawkins family fortune may allow them to cut some corners, and one of those corners might be us," Skip said.

"Never. We're too easy. Will Hawkins's views and our views are synonymous. He was fighting the ecological and economic battles long before the foundation existed. He'll claim that we adopted his beliefs and policies, not vice versa. And he would be right."

"What are you saying?" Skip asked.

"I'm saying this is all part of the plan. It's no secret to anyone that Will Hawkins has been groomed for the presidency since childhood. I just took our platform and tweaked it to complement his platform, and voilà: we trade foundation endorsement for a cabinet post if he's elected."

"You sonofabitch," Skip laughed. "How long have you been planning this?"

"About three years. But this is falling into place more quickly and effectively than I could have ever hoped."

"But what about the foundation?"

"That's the kicker, man. I take the job as energy secretary or secretary of the interior, and you take over the foundation. It's perfect."

A slow grin creased Skip's face. "Do you think he can win?"

"The planets are aligning, Skip. President Hughes is on the ropes. The economy is slipping. Ecological issues are again important to the American people. Sure, it'll be close. But with the Hawkins pocketbook behind him and the endorsement of the foundation, he's got a helluva chance. And that chance bodes well for you and me."

"You are the man!" Skip said, pumping his fist.

"Well, then, buy the man a beer."

# seven

At 7:00 a.m. in Dallas, the sun was just creeping up over the skyline as Jack McCarthy finished his second cup of coffee. The view from Jack's corner office at WPC was spectacular. He was continually amazed at the success he had achieved at WPC and never failed to savor the well-appointed environment of Dallas's largest advertising agency. Jack was proud of his success, and as he surveyed his office, he was also proud of how he had brought a personal touch to his office decoration. The pinewood furniture and distressed leather couch and chair were far from standard company issue, but they made him feel closer to his Colorado roots.

Jack smiled, remembering the first time Allen Hamilton had walked into Jack's newly decorated office.

"Jesus, who helped you decorate? Slim Pickens?"

Jack had replied, "It's a helluva lot better than your '80s Andy Warhol motif."

Jack moved over to his desk and turned his focus toward the Gen-Square pitch, by now just days away. His crash course in GenSquare's business and strategy had forced him to accumulate a load of software knowledge in just a few short weeks.

The GenSquare concept was truly revolutionary. Many analysts believed that GenSquare would supplant Microsoft as the United States's largest software provider. GenSquare's relatively inexpensive cost of entry for small businesses and consumers, coupled with its pay-as-you-use billing structure, had caught the attention of everyone— even Jack, a technically challenged advertising executive.

GenSquare was the brass ring; if WPC landed this account, Jack's status as one of the top agency executives in the country would be secure. The key was to ensure that WPC had the tiebreaker that swayed GenSquare decision makers in WPC's favor.

Jack contemplated the angles. Texas heritage wouldn't work, since both agency finalists were Dallas-based. That was too simple, anyway. What was it that the Hawkins family thrived on? Money, power, and politics. If Jack could figure out how to use any or all three of these to his advantage, he felt certain WPC could win the business.

As Jack continued to ponder this dilemma, Allen Hamilton strode into his office.

"What the fuck are you doing, Jack? We've all been in the war room for fifteen minutes, waiting on your ass."

"Shit, Allen, I'm sorry. I lost track of time. I've been here since 5:30 trying to identify the differentiator that will tip the scale in our favor. GenSquare has one; so should we." Jack grabbed his notebook, ready to hustle to WPC's main conference room.

"Sit down," Allen said. "That's an intriguing thought."

For the next forty-five minutes, Jack and Allen brainstormed about the Hawkins family hot buttons of money and politics. How could WPC exploit what the Hawkins family coveted? The answer was not a simple one, but as their ideas continued to circle around the bull's-eye, there was a feeling that they were getting somewhere. Finally, Allen suggested that the only way WPC could impact the GenSquare bottom line was by helping them sell more software.

At that moment, the light went on for Jack. "That's it, Allen!"

"What's it?"

"We base our compensation on their annual sales. We win when they win. We suffer if—and that's a big if—they suffer."

Allen sat up in his chair. "Interesting. That type of compensation structure will give that gambler Bo Hawkins a hard-on." He looked at Jack. "This is quickly becoming the best pitch we've ever assembled at WPC. But something's missing."

"I agree," Jack sighed. "IF we don't address the strategic opportunities of the campaign, even though they are not asking for it, we are missing a huge opportunity."

As the two wandered back to the war room, they agreed that they would exhaust their strategic war chest to identify the consumer insight that would catapult Will Hawkins into the most powerful office in the world. When they entered the war room, it was empty except for Carrie, who stared at them with a beady-eyed look that displayed her frustration. She knew that Allen and Jack had just hatched a key to the GenSquare pitch, and she had been left out of the discussion.

# eight

Sgt. Maj. Ian McKay moved silently through the cold, misty forest in western Wales. He and his trainees navigated the terrain, executing an exercise with the objective of identifying and eliminating an assassin targeting the prime minister. Ian, playing the part of the assassin, stealthily avoided detection by the elite guard trainees.

McKay was a pro. He had overseen so many of these exercises that, with his mind only half in the game, he could easily outmaneuver the heavily recruited trainees who were currently running around the forest like a bunch of school children.

As Sergeant McKay silently moved through the dense forest, he heard the faint crack of a twig underfoot. He stopped and listened. There he was, no more than ten feet away: the northern perimeter sentry patrolling his assigned area. Ian calculated that the facsimile of the prime minister's hunting lodge was about 350 yards west of his current position. He calmly waited in the underbrush as the sentry passed within three feet of his heavily camouflaged head and face. As the sentry turned on his heel at the east end of his patrol area, Ian waited for the perfect moment to eliminate another trainee from the exercise.

In an instant, it was over. In one move, Ian pounced on the trainee, quickly disarming the strapping young recruit and covering his mouth to avoid any inadvertent screams. The trainee slumped in the powerful arms of the stocky sergeant major, knowing he had failed his objective. The rules of the exercise stated that the trainee must acknowledge any communication transmissions for the next five minutes as if he were still in action, allowing the "assassin" time to re-establish his cover. This rule was devised to simulate the amount of time it would take a scout to investigate the break in the elite force's communication link. Ian immediately bolted back into the dense forest, moving stealthily toward the simulated hunting lodge.

The exercise continued for ninety more minutes, with trainee after unsuspecting trainee passing within feet of the sergeant major, only to be eliminated. Finally, the mock hunting lodge was less than twenty yards away, with only one more guard between Ian and his objective. He waited patiently, identifying the guard's patrol path, and then he quietly positioned himself, waiting for the opportunity to strike. It came as planned, and the final deterrent to entering the hunting lodge was eliminated.

There were two guards left, both inside the lodge. As Ian entered through the side door, it was apparent to him that the trainees inside were not expecting him to make it in. The warmth and serenity of the house had lulled them into believing that even if the sergeant major did get in the house, they would easily hear him and get to him before he got to their twenty-two-year-old classmate who was posing as the prime minister.

They were wrong. In workmanlike fashion, Ian moved from room to room of the large, rustic lodge, waiting for his opportunities. The first floor guard on his routine patrol rounded the corner to the dining room into the waiting arms of the sergeant major. It was over immediately. As the disconcerted trainee sat down on the floor, Ian gave him the patented "evil eye" that all trainees over the past twenty-one years had tried to avoid at all costs.

The last guard proved to be even simpler. He obviously didn't think it would ever come down to him versus the mock assassin. But it did, and he never knew what hit him. As Sgt. Maj. Ian McKay plucked the red flag from the hat of the "prime minister" and transmitted to the entire team that the exercise had culminated in his "assassination," each trainee was well aware that they had just been had by one of the best field operatives in the Western world. Maybe the best.

Ian's debrief of the group was scathing. Adjectives like lazy, stupid, and worthless, coupled with a significant variety of expletives, made the highly skilled trainees feel like children.

"Your collective inability to sense danger is uncanny," Ian growled. "You've got to be aware of your surroundings. You have to anticipate when danger is most likely. Every one of you treated today's exercise like a walk through Hyde Park. I am disgusted by your lack of progress."

Then Ian broke into a smile and said, "But you're the best goddamned group of young recruits I've had in years. Your mistakes today were common. Six weeks from now, you won't make the same mistakes. You'll be a finely tuned unit that will make your country proud. Now get cleaned up. Tonight we go to town before we begin our final training push. Let's meet outside the barracks at 18:30."

The trainees let out a collective cry of joy. They were getting out, albeit for only one night, of their self-imposed prison.

Later that night, as Sgt. Maj. Ian McKay and his group of highly skilled trainees sat in the Angry Dog Pub slugging back pint after pint of ales and lagers, a very different event was transpiring in Dallas, Texas. Sen. Will Hawkins stood at a podium in the family compound's library announcing his intention to seek the Democratic nomination for president of the United States. As hundreds of television cameras transmitted this news around the world, a small TV in the Angry Dog Pub in western Wales was showing the announcement.

Ian McKay was staring at the telly in a slightly dazed state of drunken bliss when he momentarily felt a hint of familiarity. What was it about the man on the screen? He felt as if he knew him.

Then all at once it came back to him. He stood, silently pointing at the screen, knocking over his bar stool. While that got everyone's attention, no one knew what he knew.

That was the man who had killed his little brother so long ago.

# nine

The *Dallas Free Press* was one of the premier newspapers in the country. With the early '90s demise of its mortal enemy, *The Dallas Times Herald*, the *Free Press* had established a newspaper monopoly in a market with roughly five million captive readers. Robert Chambers was the editor-in-chief and publisher of the *Free Press*. Though small in stature at only 5'5", he made up for that lack of first impression with his fiery personality and determination.

Chambers was used to getting his way. On this beautiful September morning, in his weekly staff meeting, what Chambers wanted was for Greg Larson, his extremely independent Pulitzer Prize–winning journalist, to cover from start to finish the presidential run of Dallas's own William S. Hawkins.

As the staff discussed the merits of an ongoing feature story of this type, Tom Johnson, managing editor and Greg Larson's boss, was quick to point out that Larson wasn't going to like this idea one bit. "He hates the idea of people telling him what to write about. And he hates even more the idea of being assigned to a story that doesn't have the intrinsic potential to shock John Q. Public."

"But this is the story of a lifetime, Tom," Chambers responded. "Anatomy of a presidential campaign. Big-time money. Big-time politics. The friggin' Hawkins family, for God's sake! What else could he want?" Johnson remained silent.

The phone on the conference table nearest Chambers rang. Chambers answered. "Yes, all right, send him in." He looked intently at Johnson and said, "Your boy Larson is on his way up. Do me a favor; make this happen."

Johnson sighed. He knew that Chambers wasn't actually viewing it as a favor; it was a mandate.

As Greg Larson entered the conference room, Stacy, Chambers's newest assistant, let out an audible sigh. Larson was quite handsome. A thirty-seven-year-old bachelor, Larson was in better shape today than he had been on his University of Missouri graduation day. A three-time All–Big 12 point guard, Larson's tenacious reputation on the basketball court had been adequately exceeded by his pit-bull reputation as an investigative journalist.

Larson confidently strode to the nearest empty chair at the conference table, seated himself, calmly leaned back, and asked, "What's up, Tom?"

Johnson leaned toward Larson and stated, "We've got the story of the year for you, Greg."

"Yeah, like I've never heard that before. What is it?"

Johnson glanced briefly at his editor-in-chief, then launched in. "It's covering Will Hawkins's run for president. It's got all the right elements: local interest, national interest, money, and big-time politics. We need your name to legitimize the series, Greg."

Larson surveyed the *Free Press* elite. "You all know this isn't my kind of story. Where's the intrigue? Where's the injustice?"

As Johnson began to respond, Greg raised his hand for silence.

"But I'll do it, on one condition. I want editorial oversight of the series. Everything I write gets printed."

"No problem!" Chambers exclaimed. "We've never edited your work before. Why would we start now?"

"I've never done a story on the most powerful family in Texas before," Greg said. "And there's a possibility that, as a Jack Nicholson character once said, 'You can't handle the truth.'"

"Try me," Chambers barked.

"I will, Robert. I think there are plenty of skeletons in the Hawkins closet, and I plan on uncovering a few."

With that, Chambers's staff meeting adjourned.

# ten

The group was seated around Will Hawkins's office conference table in a posh office tower in Dallas. It wasn't the trendiest office address in Dallas, but Will's 2,000-square-foot office on the forty-first floor had to be one of the most stunning anywhere. The room featured a natural wood interior coupled with custom-made furniture that was somewhere between Ralph Lauren and Ethan Allen, which made it a very comfortable workspace with a view looking out over the Crescent and onto Highland Park and North Dallas. The conference table seated twelve and was as rustic as they come. It had once served as the mess table for the 10th Mountain Division that trained near Vail, Colorado, during World War II.

The conference table was half full. John Rollins and Pete Robinson, Will's key advisers, were among the attendees. The task of the day was to finalize the framework of Will Hawkins's campaign strategy. The opinions varied, but it was clear that Will was in control. They all felt that they were making progress when Stephanie Wood, Will's Dallas-based administrative assistant of more than ten years, politely knocked on the door. She discreetly motioned to Will that she needed to see him in her own spacious, well-decorated outer office.

When Will strode through the door, Stephanie said, "David Ellis is on hold for you. I thought you would want to take the call."

Stephanie made it her business to know what calls Mr. Hawkins would want to take and which ones she would politely take a message for. As usual, her instincts were dead on; Will looked stunned.

He returned to his office and dismissed the entire strategic team. "I've got a very important call I must take. Let's reconvene after lunch. Sorry for the inconvenience."

As the group left the office, John Rollins eyed Will suspiciously. Will winked at Rollins, trying to put his mind at ease. When the group was gone and the office door shut behind them, Will picked up the phone.

"Mr. Ellis, what an unexpected surprise."

"Cut the bull, Senator Hawkins. You knew I would call."

"I have no idea what you are talking about, sir, but I don't appreciate being spoken to in that tone of voice."

"I apologize, Senator, but I don't appreciate being patronized, either."

"Fair enough, Mr. Ellis. Let's start over. What can I do for you?"

"I believe," responded Ellis, "it's what we can do for each other."

"Really," Will sighed noncommittally. "And what might that be?"

"I'm calling to suggest an alliance," Ellis stated. "A mutually beneficial one. I don't for a minute want you to believe that I like your politics or your style. But we do have a common enemy in the president."

"Enemy is a strong word, Mr. Ellis. I prefer opponent," Will said.

"Very well, opponent. But the point is, President Hughes is destroying our country. His lack of economic vision, his lax ecological policies, his reduction of funding for the war on drugs . . . it's slowly and relentlessly bringing us down."

"I agree," Will said, "but what does that have to do with you and me?"

"Well," David responded, "in a nutshell, I pledge the foundation's support to your campaign, and in return you commit to real economic and ecological change, a return to a full-scale war on drugs, and, oh—a post for me in your cabinet."

"Well, Mr. Ellis, the commitment to real change is an easy one. That has been my platform for the past eight years. In fact, I've always believed your foundation was guilty of a little plagiarism, if you want to know the truth. But the cabinet post is a little tougher. I'll have to visit with my advisers on that subject."

"The choice is yours, Senator," David said. "I'd just hate to have to pledge our support in a different direction."

As they exchanged goodbyes, both men were very pleased with themselves. Will couldn't believe the good luck that had just graced his luxurious office; David knew he had just reeled in the biggest fish of his career.

# eleven

It was a beautiful October morning in Dallas, as each morning had been for the past three weeks. Jack McCarthy was on his third cup of coffee as the sun began to rise.

Today was the day. At 10:00 sharp, the GenSquare new-business pitch would begin. It was the most important day of business in Jack's illustrious career and also the most important day in the history of WPC.

As Jack strolled down the long, richly paneled executive hall toward the boardroom, the butterflies he felt before any big presentation began to assemble in his stomach. Jack smiled, remembering what Allen Hamilton had said about prepresentation jitters. "Everyone gets butterflies," Allen had told him. "The question is whether you can get them to fly in formation."

Jack knew that a stellar performance today was a lock. He'd practiced his presentation hundreds of times. The agency had spared no expense in getting the team ready. They were as prepared today as they would ever be.

Jack entered the boardroom and was once again awed by the magnitude and thoroughness of WPC's organization for today's presentation. The entire room had been converted into an interactive extravaganza; it looked like an Apple store, featuring every new product they had to offer. Each piece of technical hardware had been wirelessly connected to the GenSquare software product. The entire WPC presentation could be viewed on individual monitors by the attendees sitting around the boardroom table. The walls of the boardroom were adorned with oversized copies of the best print work the agency had ever produced. And the TV reel WPC's creative team had assembled would be the envy of every other agency in the country. WPC was ready. Jack was ready. Only two more hours until showtime.

Jack was seated at the end of the boardroom table as his colleagues arrived. One by one, the best and brightest the agency had to offer took their seats around the table. Allen Hamilton was the last to arrive. He walked to the front of the room. All eyes were upon him. It seemed like an eternity before he began to speak.

"Ladies and gentlemen, this is the day we've all been waiting for. This is the moment in time that will define who we are for the rest of our careers. I am proud of how well we've prepared. But all of this hard work will mean nothing if we don't get the business. So, don't sit around the table and gloat about the great product we've created. Bear down. Concentrate. Execute. It's first and goal at the one-yard line. But we don't win if we don't score. Each and every one of you will play a key role in whether we succeed or fail. Do your job. Do it like we practiced. Let's bring home the trophy."

As Jack listened to Allen, he realized this was a special moment; he was listening to the best Knute Rockne speech anyone at WPC had ever heard. And as he looked around the table, he knew they were going to win. He saw the fire in the eyes of his colleagues. Winning was the only option.

"Everybody take a deep breath," Allen said as he concluded. "I want you to relax as much as you can. We're an hour away from the presentation; your brains need some down time, and your bodies need some fuel. I have a light brunch set up in my conference room. Get something to eat. Try to talk about something other than GenSquare. Be back here at 9:45 sharp." The GenSquare team filed out of the boardroom and left Allen alone with his thoughts.

At 10:03 the elevator doors of WPC opened, and the GenSquare contingent stepped into the lobby. The group was led by Bo Hawkins, followed closely by Will Hawkins and three other members of Gen-Square leadership. They were taken to the boardroom, where the WPC team had been waiting for nearly twenty minutes. The introductions were brief and slightly strained. It was apparent that the GenSquare team had decided in advance to avoid any prolonged small talk.

Allen Hamilton began the presentation. He talked about WPC as comfortably as he would his own family. He touched on capabilities. He described the biographies of his colleagues around the table. It never ceased to amaze Jack just how simple Allen made it look. Allen ended his introduction with WPC's Texas heritage. It was obvious that this struck a chord with Bo Hawkins and his Texas wildcatter mentality.

Next, Scott Parks presented the agency's research findings, along with the corresponding product positioning and creative strategy. The GenSquare people appeared to be impressed. Then came Sharon Campbell, who presented the digital approach and media plan. Again, this portion of the presentation was greeted with approving nods, although Bo Hawkins didn't appear to agree with the spending levels proposed.

Following the media portion of the presentation, Dana Howard, one of the most notable creative talents in the US, outlined WPC's concept for the GenSquare creative campaign. While she was very polished and entertaining, Allen and Jack exchanged looks, because it was evident that the GenSquare people around the table were not reacting as positively as they had been to the previous segments of the presentation. When Dana sat down, Allen gave Jack the "time to save the day" look.

Jack began by summarizing the presentation. He outlined the strength of WPC's research, positioning, media, and creative presentations. Jack paused to lend emphasis to what he planned to say next. "But despite all we've shown you so far, we know that may not be enough to win your business."

Allen grimaced as Jack continued. "We know you've been meeting with some of the best agencies in the country. We're humble enough to acknowledge that you're probably looking for that little extra something." Again Jack paused. "We believe we have it. And it comes in two packages."

Allen was now clearly nervous. He knew that Jack planned to unveil the proposed WPC compensation structure, but what else did he have up his sleeve? Jack spotted Allen's uneasiness but plunged ahead.

"Our first tiebreaker is financial in nature. GenSquare is a startup company. While it has the power of the Hawkins family behind it, it still has financial goals to meet. And with the significant marketing costs associated with competing in this category, we believe we should share in the financial burden of getting started. So our proposal is quite simple: We don't make money until you do. We've created a fee arrangement that covers our costs to service your business, but our profit only starts when yours does. We would also propose a bonus clause that allows us to recapture previously lost profits once GenSquare achieves the fair share of profits we all know it will."

Jack's comments were met with silence, but the look on Bo Hawkins's face told him that he had made a positive impact.

Now it was time for Jack to unveil the second tiebreaker idea. He knew he was living on the edge, especially with Allen Hamilton. But to win big, Jack had always believed you had to take risks. So he launched in. "We've also been thinking about Senator Hawkins's campaign."

Allen winced, not knowing what was coming next.

"It appears to us," Jack said, "that while the Democratic nomination is a lock, it will be a pretty tight race with President Hughes."

With that, Allen Hamilton interrupted. "Mr. Hawkins," Allen addressed Bo, "when Jack references us, he actually means him. We at WPC have obviously discussed Senator Hawkins's campaign but have never arrived at an agency point of view. So I would like to suggest—"

Bo Hawkins raised his hand for silence and said, "Let the young man speak."

Allen fell back in his chair.

"As I was about to say," Jack continued, "Senator Hawkins's platform addresses so many of the concerns raised by today's Americans: economy, ecology, drugs. People are concerned about their children's future, their country's future. Then it dawned on me: The Hawkins platform of the last eight years, and the reason I'm personally passionate about the campaign, has shocking similarities to the platform of the grassroots organization The Future State Foundation. I suggest—and I won't say 'we,' Allen—that the Hawkins campaign and the foundation form an alliance. It gives you access to an up-and-down-the-street organization that can help you campaign. It gives them a viable presidential candidate who's passionate about their issues." As Jack paused, Bo Hawkins interrupted.

"Young man, you are obviously passionate about your business and your politics. I hate to cut you short, but our time is tight, and I've got an afternoon schedule to keep. So Allen, if you wouldn't mind giving us a few minutes?"

"Certainly, Mr. Hawkins," Allen responded.

The WPC team filed out of the boardroom.

When they were clearly out of earshot of the boardroom, Allen turned to Jack and said, "What the fuck do you think you're doing? We had Hawkins with the compensation deal, and then you go off the reservation and ad lib your own political viewpoints. If we lose this account, I'm holding you personally responsible."

The rest of the WPC team refused to make eye contact with either Jack or Allen, with the exception of Carrie, who was looking at Jack the way a mother looks at a sick child. The silence was deafening. The WPC team was stunned by Jack's actions and Allen's reaction. The next five minutes seemed like an eternity, and no one said a word.

Jack finally spoke up. "Allen, I did what I thought was right. I knew you'd never let me say what I said, so I didn't ask permission. If we don't get the account, I'll resign. If we get it, you owe me a big fucking apology."

That statement shocked everyone present. Carrie looked proud of Jack's response.

All Allen said was, "Deal."

Just then one of Bo Hawkins's entourage came out of the boardroom and called the WPC team back in.

Once everyone was settled, Bo Hawkins addressed Hamilton. "Allen, your presentation was fantastic. The efforts behind your recommendations were very apparent. Your compensation proposal was innovative and compelling. And Jack McCarthy's political instincts are uncanny.

"Allen, I have a proposal for you. GenSquare believes you are the agency partner for us. As of this moment we are awarding you the account. Additionally, while your compensation package is intriguing, we are not interested in your proposed arrangement. We don't want anything getting in the way of your commitment to our business, so we would prefer to pay you under a more typical arrangement. But I do have one favor to ask."

"Anything," Allen beamed.

"We would like WPC to lend us Jack McCarthy as the consumer adviser on Will's campaign."

Allen responded, "I'd obviously say yes in a heartbeat, Mr. Hawkins, but that's really up to Jack."

Bo turned toward Jack. "What do you say, Jack?"

Jack paused for what seemed like a minute. "I'd be honored, sir."

# twelve

Sgt. Maj. Ian McKay sat alone at the one-hundred-year-old bar. In his drunken stupor he stared at the names and dates, some dating back before World War I, carved into the wood. Ian was a mess. He hadn't eaten or slept since the moment he made the connection that Sen. Will Hawkins, more than likely the next US president, was the same man who had killed his brother in a bar brawl years ago. But he had no idea what to do about it, so he drank.

McKay was in hot water with his superiors. He'd missed training sessions with his unit and meetings with his next in command, and their patience with this highly decorated career soldier was wearing painfully thin. But he couldn't shake the ghost.

Ian was hell-bent on revenge, but how? He could obviously retire with full pension after his long, distinguished career, but then what? Will Hawkins would be well guarded, and doing harm to Hawkins wouldn't really solve anything anyway. Ian's thoughts wandered back to his niece, Lizzie, the daughter of his dead brother, Sean. Sean had never even known his girlfriend, Patricia, was pregnant. And over the years of Lizzie's life, Ian had fantasized on and off about what he would do to the guy who had stolen her father's life. Now he had found him.

Lizzie's life had been hard. Neither Patricia's family nor the McKays had much money. It was difficult for Patricia to get good work as a single mother and even more difficult to find a man who wanted an instant family. So Ian took on the role of surrogate father and gave them as much financial support as he could afford on his meager salary.

At that moment, pondering their financial difficulties, everything became crystal clear. Ian decided that the revenge he would extract was financial. He would hit Sen. Will Hawkins where it would hurt him the most: in the wallet. With that, Ian ordered another pint, stared out the window at the gloomy afternoon, and began to develop his plan of blackmail and revenge.

○ ○ ○

At the same moment, more than three thousand miles away, Jack and Carrie lay in his bed, discussing the future.

"I can't believe that you're actually going through with it," Carrie said, annoyed. "You're dismantling the best new-business team in the Southwest to work on a political campaign. They must be paying you a ton of money to put your career on hold like this."

"Actually, they're not," Jack responded, "but Allen is subsidizing my salary to keep me as a WPC advocate."

Carrie scoffed. "Is that even ethical?"

Jack laughed, "Ethical isn't a word in Allen's vocabulary. You know that."

"But what about you, Jack? That's not your style."

"Well, to be perfectly honest, I already cleared it with Will Hawkins, and he thought it was a great idea. Because campaign expenses are made public, he couldn't pay me more than others on the campaign team, and in his mind, this ensures that I don't have second thoughts and lose focus over the next year."

"I still don't understand, Jack."

"I'm not sure I do either. But I do know Will Hawkins is passionate about the same things I am. I haven't been this excited about marketing a product in years. Maybe ever."

After a few minutes of silence, Carrie asked, "What happens if he loses, Jack? Do you really believe Allen will take you back?"

"I'm not sure. But I've rationalized to myself that if I make a good impression on the Hawkins family, win or lose, Allen won't have much choice."

Again quiet. It was Jack's turn to break the silence. "I have to be honest, Carrie. My biggest concern is losing you. Our paths over the next year are going to be quite divergent, and whether I've done a good job of communicating it or not, I've become quite fond of you."

"Fond!" Carrie laughed nervously. "Is that the best you can do? I was hoping this was the moment you would profess your undying love for me."

"I am," Jack whined. "I'm just not very good at it."

They both laughed. Then, without warning, the passion each felt toward the other pulled them together in an intense embrace. After what seemed like an eternity, they looked into each other's eyes and connected in the depths of their souls.

They made love as if they'd never see each other again. When they came back to earth, Jack realized he was running late for his first day as the consumer strategist on the Will Hawkins campaign. He quickly showered, dressed, kissed Carrie on the forehead, and was gone.

Carrie lay there for a while, wondering what was in store for them. Jack was the best thing that had ever happened to her, and she had a nagging feeling that his new position was not necessarily going to be good for them.

# thirteen

J ack arrived at campaign headquarters at 9:10. The first person he saw as he entered the palatial forty-first floor of the Hawkins Oil Tower was John Rollins, Senator Hawkins's campaign chief of staff.

"Jesus, McCarthy, it's your first day on the job and you're late. I don't know what type of hours you keep in the advertising business, but this job is 24/7. Now let's get over to the conference room. The research geeks are giving us an update on where we stand."

John Rollins stood about 5'6" in his lifts, and his high-pitched East Texas twang was enough to make anyone's skin crawl. He also was one of the most successful bankers in Texas, and Jack knew he had a personal and professional relationship with Bo Hawkins that went back twenty-five years. His reputation was what legends were made of. He never took no for an answer, absolutely hated to lose, and never let anything get in the way of achieving his objective. And currently, his objective was getting Will Hawkins elected as the next president of the United States. Jack followed Rollins into the conference room. Around the table sat one of the most formidable campaign teams ever assembled. Jack felt an adrenaline rush, just being part of this group.

Once the introductions were complete, the pollsters began their analysis of the National Opinion Poll. More than a thousand surveys were conducted weekly to identify a candidate's current position in the race to become the Democratic candidate as well as his position relative to the current president, Robert F. Hughes. The numbers didn't lie; Will Hawkins's awareness and preference ratings were increasing, but at a snail's pace.

"If this trend continues," Doug Evans, the campaign's research director said, "we'll have to double our advertising budget just to have a prayer."

The room was silent. No one had expected it to be this difficult.

"Thank you for such an uplifting analysis of the numbers, Mr. Evans," John Rollins said. "You can be seated now."

Then Rollins proceeded to attack every person in the room. He started with Steve Bess, the campaign's assistant chief of staff and Rollins's right-hand man for the past fifteen years. He saved Jack for last.

"Well, Mr. McCarthy, I'm glad you could make it this morning. You were ten minutes late on your first day, and you're four weeks late for why we hired you. Where the fuck is this consumer expertise we were promised? We need results, and as all of you have probably noticed, we don't have them. Now, I'm going to leave before I get really pissed. But before this day is done, I expect a plan from each of you on how we're going to accelerate the national popularity of Senator Hawkins."

Rollins then spun on his heel, stormed out the door, and slammed it behind him.

The room was eerily silent. Steve Bess spoke first. "All right, people, you know the drill. Doug, need your thoughts on the regional skew of the numbers. Chris, rerun the budget numbers and give me a 10 percent increase in our TV media budget. Kim, update the status on volunteer recruitment. Lie if you have to; I need increases. The rest of you get back to work. Jack, you come with me."

When Jack and Steve entered Bess's office, Steve quickly shut the door behind them. "Well, Jack," Steve said, chuckling, "how're you enjoying the new job?"

Jack took a deep breath. "Holy shit, that guy's a maniac."

"Yeah, he is," Steve replied, "and I should know. I've been working with him for fifteen years. But don't take it personally; that's his definition of motivation. And you know what? It works on most people."

"But that bullshit about me being four weeks late! I didn't set the start date; that was Bo Hawkins's call."

"I know that, Jack. Rollins knows it too. He's just giving you a little kick-start by sticking his boot right up your ass." Both men laughed.

"Listen, Jack," Bess continued, "John Rollins is a winner, whether you like his methods or not. We both worked on Will Hawkins's senate campaign and were rewarded by getting to keep the Hawkins account at Metroplex Bank. Now we're in the Super Bowl, and John Rollins will not accept the possibility of losing. He's Ross Perot, Vince Lombardi, and Attila the Hun all rolled into one. But he's manageable if you know the buttons to push, and I do. So stick close by me until you get more comfortable. Now, I've got a shitload to get done today, but let's get a drink after work, and we can discuss next steps regarding your consumer strategy."

Jack agreed and left Steve Bess's office knowing he'd just made a new friend. And just as importantly, he'd identified the ally that would help him navigate the waters of this shark tank they called a campaign.

# fourteen

John Rollins and Will Hawkins sat in silence across the large coffee table from each other. Will Hawkins's spacious downtown office had become the unofficial campaign war room where many of the real strategic decisions of the campaign were made. On this beautiful fall afternoon, they were discussing the various polls that indicated Will's popularity was not climbing quickly enough.

Rollins broke the silence with a pitch in his voice that was higher than normal. "I've asked Steve Bess to revisit many of the key components of the campaign and have recommendations to me by end of day. But that's not going to be enough. We need a giant boost. We need to announce the alliance with The Future State Foundation. We need David Ellis to go to the media and announce his support for the Will Hawkins campaign for president. It needs to be one of those fiery, passionate speeches that motivates the masses and makes the girls swoon. We can use all the female voters we can get."

"I agree," Will said, "but even that might not be enough. We have to do something big. Something that will catapult us to the front of the pack."

"Got any bright ideas?"

Will shot him a dirty look and said, "As a matter of fact, I do. I've been going over this in my mind for days, and I think I've come up with a plan."

"Well, come on, what gives?"

"John, whatever is said in this office is strictly confidential, right?"

"Of course, Will. Our objectives are 100 percent aligned. Now, what's the idea?"

"I'm not sure where to start, so I'll go from the very beginning. The genesis of this idea came while I was pondering the weaknesses of President Hughes. I think we all believe I can win the Democratic candidacy. It's beating Hughes and his fucking impenetrable approval ratings that have us worried."

"I agree. Go on."

"So the key to accelerating my poll numbers is to capitalize on a weakness of the president. Now, my key platforms of economy, ecology, and drugs are all relative weaknesses of the current administration. Having any significant impact on the economy or the war on drugs is beyond our control. But people's ecological concerns offer some interesting opportunities."

"I'm not sure I understand," Rollins said. "Cleaning up the environment and passing meaningful legislation aimed at industries not in compliance with current environmental acts is every bit as difficult to impact as the other two."

"I agree," Will smiled, "but you're missing the simpler avenue. We don't focus on fixing the problem. We focus on making it a bigger problem for President Hughes."

Rollins looked puzzled and for a rare moment was speechless.

Will continued, "A few strategically placed environmental mishaps, and President Hughes has a shitload of bad press on his hands. That, coupled with a few heartfelt and passionate speeches regarding the legacy we are creating for our children and, voilà! Chinks in the presidential armor and arrows in the Will Hawkins quiver. Not to mention a huge motivator for David Ellis to get vocal about Will Hawkins as America's agent of change."

Rollins was stunned but intrigued. "But how do you propose we make these incidents happen without you—or should I say us—getting dirty?"

"It's actually simpler than it sounds," Will said, smiling. "Did I ever tell you who my college roommate was?"

"No, as a matter of fact, you didn't."

"Carlos Pendrill."

"The Carlos Pendrill? The Mexican financier and drug cartel leader? Jesus, Will, when were you planning on springing this one on me? That type of surprise could really hurt us!"

"Now, John, I know it's not optimal, but his family was not suspected of drug trafficking at that time, and it's not like we play golf together on weekends. In fact, we haven't spoken in over ten years."

"So what does he have to do with the ecological undermining of President Hughes?"

"Well, when we graduated from Oxford, we did a little bar-hopping the night before we both came back to this side of the pond."

Will explained about the night in the bar, the ensuing fight, and how he had most assuredly saved Carlos Pendrill, now the most powerful and feared man in Mexico, from being beaten to death in the alley behind a London pub.

"So you see, John, Carlos Pendrill owes me one. My repayment for saving his life is a few well-placed environmental accidents carried out by his people. Hughes won't know what hit him."

Smiling, Will Hawkins leaned back in his chair, clearly proud of his elaborate plan. John Rollins was silent for several moments, obviously pondering the monumental risk to what had just been laid out before him.

When he finally spoke, it was three simple words: "Let's do it."

o o o

At the same moment, in *The Dallas Free Press* headquarters on the other side of downtown, Greg Larson and Tom Johnson were meeting in Johnson's office.

"I'm telling you, Tom," Larson complained, "this series is going nowhere. I can't find a thing on Will Hawkins. No affairs, no tax problems. They even pay Social Security tax on their maids and yard people. This guy's obviously known for a long time that he was going to run for president. I really believed that the legendary ruthlessness and drive of the Hawkins family would turn up some scandal to liven up this campaign."

"Maybe it's just legend," Tom Johnson responded.

"I don't buy it, Tom. I've always believed there was something fishy about the Hawkins family, and I should be the investigative reporter to uncover it."

"Well, regardless of whether you uncover any dirt on Will Hawkins or not, this campaign is big news in Dallas, and I'd like you to continue. Not to mention that you all but guaranteed Chambers a newsworthy breakthrough." Johnson shrugged and broke into a big grin.

"I'll continue, but I need help, Tom."

"Name it."

"I want a full-time researcher assigned to me. I want to uncover the shady dealings that I'm convinced exist within the confines of the Hawkins family compound."

Johnson, relieved by the simple nature of the request, quickly agreed. He was ecstatic to be keeping his best reporter on the biggest story in Dallas since 1963.

# fifteen

Will Hawkins's campaign numbers were slowly climbing, but at a rate that had the pollsters predicting Hawkins could not overtake President Hughes and win the general election. Jack McCarthy was concerned, and he channeled that concern into what he knew best: identifying a strategic insight that would make a product more appealing to consumers. As Jack flew on the Hawkins's private jet from market to market, he conducted a grueling series of quantitative research studies, focus groups, and one-on-one interviews. His findings were not identifying anything new or insightful. But they had confirmed that the American public, while supportive of President Hughes, believed that the current administration was neglecting the environment and the war on drugs.

When Jack arrived at Dallas Love Field in the Hawkins Gulfstream V, he'd only slept four of the past forty-eight hours. But rather than go home for a nap, he called Will Hawkins's administrative assistant, Stephanie Wood, to request the earliest possible opening on Hawkins's extremely busy calendar. After a few moments of delay, Stephanie returned to the line. "Jack, Mr. Hawkins says he can see you in ninety minutes. The limo should be there in a few minutes, so I guess you'll have some time to kill. I could meet you at Capitol Grill for a quick lunch if you're interested."

Jack was starving but thought better of being seen at the trendy Dallas eatery with Will Hawkins's very attractive assistant. The press, not to mention Carrie's nosey friends, would have a field day if the two of them were spotted together. This also wasn't the first time Stephanie had shown interest in Jack. It would be prudent not to encourage her.

"It sounds great, Stephanie, but if I'm going to be meeting with the future president of the United States, a shower is probably the smart plan."

They both laughed, and Jack signed off by saying he'd see her around 1:15.

When Jack entered Will Hawkins's plush office, the candidate was talking in hushed tones on one of his three desktop telephones. He casually motioned for Jack to sit on one of the couches on the opposite side of the office. Jack strolled casually to the window looking out on the Crescent and beyond.

When Will Hawkins ended his call, he immediately asked, "What do you have for me, Jack? I need a boost this afternoon."

"Well, sir, there's not much new to report."

"Jack, I would prefer if you called me Will. I'm not that much older than you are. Secondly, I need news. You've been on our plane for the past ten days crisscrossing the country, and I need something fresh."

"Well, Will, I believe we have something fresh, something new."

"Go on."

"Our research confirms that your platform is consistent with the American people's concerns. Ecological naiveté and lip service relating to the war on drugs are the issues that are top-of-mind. Will, it's time to announce your alliance with The Future State Foundation. Endorsement and support from David Ellis, focusing on all the issues but with special emphasis on the environment and drugs, should have a significant impact on America's view of the Hughes and Hawkins campaigns."

"I agree, Jack. And as a matter of fact, David Ellis and I are meeting in three days to map out the announcement. I was concerned that I might alienate certain constituencies, but your work over the past week validates that my concerns are unwarranted."

Jack was stunned.

"I don't know what to say. I thought I was coming in here to convince you of the merits of the alliance. Instead, you're three days away from finalizing it. I feel like an idiot."

"Not at all, Jack. I've been forging ahead because I was concerned that Ray Langston, our naïve Democratic competitor from Oregon, might beat me to the punch. Your research over the past ten days has provided me a shitload of confidence that this alliance is exactly what my campaign needs. Now, I know you've been killing yourself ever since you started here, so take a couple of days off and be here fresh and ready for our meeting with David Ellis."

"Really?" Jack knew he was an integral player in the development of the campaign's strategy, but he never expected to be included in the meeting.

"I appreciate the invitation, Will, and I won't embarrass you."

"I know you won't, Jack. Now, if you don't mind, I have a couple of calls to make."

Jack and Will shook hands, and Jack let himself out of the office. Walking down the hallway, he pulled out his cell phone to see if he could coax Carrie out of the office early for drinks, dinner, and a quiet evening alone.

o o o

After Jack had left, Will Hawkins sat pondering what it would be like to sit alone in the Oval Office as the most powerful person in the world. The thought sent chills down his spine. But just as quickly as the daydream began, it ended with a more sobering thought—what if he lost? Once again, Will Hawkins remembered what he'd known for years: Losing was not something he could deal with or ever even contemplate. He had to do whatever it took to win the presidency. The decision was final: Carlos Pendrill was the necessary evil that would help ensure his victory.

# sixteen

Will Hawkins and Carlos Pendrill sat in the large open living area of the Hawkins ranch in Ozona, Texas. Wildcat Ranch, aptly named by Bo Hawkins nearly thirty years ago, had served many purposes over the years: hosting family holiday getaways; a hunting lodge for the senior Hawkins, his friends, and business associates; and a clandestine meeting ground for rendezvous that were best kept out of the press. On a blustery autumn afternoon, a meeting was taking place there that both participants were most anxious to keep out of the public eye.

As Will and Carlos exchanged pleasantries and stories from their college days, the well-appointed, rustic ranch house seemed to be absorbing the gravity of the moment. When both men appeared to have run out of small talk, Carlos Pendrill took the direct approach. "Will, it really is great to see you, but I'm tired of waiting to hear why you asked me here. What is so important and secretive that you send a rented plane to Mexico City to fly me to this beautiful home in the most god-forsaken portion of the Texas outback?"

Will remained quiet. As the two men stared at each other, Carlos was obviously getting annoyed. Finally, Will broke the silence. "Carlos,

I've asked you here to do me a favor. Not just any favor; this is a monumental favor."

"So what do you need, my friend?"

"Well, let me give you a little background. We're not worried about winning the Democratic nomination. But once we match up with President Hughes, we don't think we'll fare as well. And since you probably don't follow my political career all that closely . . . "

"Ah, but I do, Will. I actually follow your career quite closely," Carlos said.

"I'm flattered, Carlos, but what I am getting at is that my campaign platforms are consistent with the leadership the American people want. These platforms also identify a relative weakness in the current administration. What I need is some help in accelerating the public awareness of this weakness in an effort to quickly surpass President Hughes in the public opinion polls."

"And that's where I come in."

"Correct. I need your organization to execute a few mishaps resulting in some newsworthy ecological events that will reinforce my current platforms and capitalize on my yet-to-be-announced alliance with David Ellis and his Future State Foundation."

The room fell silent. The only sounds were coming from outside where the hands on the working ranch were putting an end to another day.

When Carlos finally spoke, his voice was firm and direct. "I'm willing to consider your proposal, but my participation will not come without some reciprocal favors."

"What about the favor of saving your life in London?" Will asked.

"I will never forget that night, Will. But what you are asking today could jeopardize everything I have worked so hard to build."

Disgusted, Will responded, "What type of favors would you be looking for?"

"I would like to develop an arrangement where my product shipments find an easier path to my US distributors."

"You mean I simplify your drug-smuggling operation? You must be out of your fucking mind! An agreement like that flies in the face of everything I stand for and believe. I will not stoop to that level."

"But you're willing to stoop to ecological terrorism to get elected. Seems somewhat hypocritical, don't you think?" Carlos had a slight sneer on his face.

"Fuck off, Carlos. Hundreds of thousands of people, mostly kids, die by your hand each year. My solution is not intended to kill anyone."

"You're so naïve, Will. Any disaster of the magnitude necessary to warrant national press coverage will include some incidental human sacrifice. You need big disasters to generate big news. So get tough or stop wasting my time. And just one point of clarification," Carlos continued. "Drug users die by their own hand, not mine. I'm simply a businessman dealing in the real world of supply and demand. And if I don't supply it, someone else will."

Again the ranch house was quiet. "I can't do it, Carlos. Even if I wanted to, I'm not sure I could."

"Well, I guess that ends our little reunion," Carlos said, standing. "I wish you the best in your efforts to become the next US president. Oh, and by the way, if I see an increased effort to crack down on my enterprise while you're in office, I'll make sure this private conversation becomes very public."

Will stared at Pendrill. "Carlos, wait. I'm sure we can work something out. What if we plant one of your key lieutenants on the Drug Enforcement Council? Then you'll have an insider who will have much more impact than I could have personally. And it also maintains the proper distance between us."

"That's an interesting suggestion, Will. Now, you see? I knew we could reach some sort of mutually beneficial arrangement," Carlos said, smiling and sitting back down.

For the next hour, Will and Carlos discussed the types of events that would maximize impact and news coverage. The events they discussed were on a much larger scale than Will had originally envisioned but on a scale that was, in both their minds, ultimately necessary. The number of accidents was also discussed. One tragedy would be seen as just an isolated accident, two, a terrible coincidence. Three would generate the type of news coverage that would significantly benefit the campaign. But four unrelated, yet tragic, ecological disasters would spawn a worldwide outrage that President Hughes could never recover from.

As they talked, a corner of Will's mind recoiled at how this had gotten so big, so fast. Yes, it was his idea to create some ecological hurdles for President Hughes, but his visions of hurdles were nothing like what he found himself agreeing to at this very moment.

When the two men were through with their discussion, Carlos told Will, "Now you must trust me and let me do my work. We should minimize contact to ensure neither of us is ever linked to these coincidental accidents."

"I agree," Will stated, "but I must know the final plan in order to fully capitalize on the opportunity. You can always reach me on my secure office phone at this number." Will handed Carlos a slip of paper.

The two men stood, and after an awkward pause they hugged, knowing that they would probably never see each other again.

As the stretch Suburban transported Carlos back to the Wildcat Ranch's private airstrip, Carlos Pendrill couldn't help but laugh out loud. The naiveté of Will Hawkins amazed him. Soon he would be in control of the next president of the United States.

○ ○ ○

At that same moment in a small, dingy office in Portland, Oregon, Ray Langston, Will Hawkins's chief Democratic competitor, was meeting with his top aides. Langston was a native Oregonian, a high school and college track star, and a Rhodes Scholar. He had chosen politics as his career to make a difference. His current position as minority whip in the US House of Representatives had catapulted him to the top of the Democratic candidate list . . . but that was prior to the entry of Will Hawkins.

Langston was a visionary politician. He too was very concerned with environmental issues and had a well-thought-out vision regarding the economic direction the country should take in the coming years. But today's conversation wasn't centered on either of those two subjects. Today's subject was money. The Langston campaign budget was extremely tight, and the group sitting around the conference room table was discussing the options.

"I just don't see how we can keep up," claimed an exasperated John Baxter, Langston's campaign chief.

"I agree," added another Langston aide. "The Hawkins pockets are just too deep."

Langston silently leaned back in his chair. He asked, "Are you telling me we should throw in the towel?" His question was met with silence and the bowing of heads. "I guess that's answer enough," he said. "Well, gentlemen, it's disappointing that we weren't even able to fight the good fight, but I'd have to agree. We just don't have the resources to compete with Hawkins. And while he and I have had our differences over the years, I do believe his policies and mine have more consistencies than differences. So if you are all in agreement, I'll make the announcement tomorrow that we're pulling out of the race and throwing our support to the Hawkins camp."

Langston's aides silently left the conference room, leaving him alone with his thoughts. As Langston pondered the situation, he cursed Will Hawkins's family money and the fact that his race to the Oval Office was over before it ever got started.

# seventeen

Carlos Pendrill and Jorge Castilla, his confidante, bodyguard, and enforcer, were sitting in the study of Pendrill's Mexico City mansion discussing the meeting Carlos had just attended at Wildcat Ranch. As Carlos recounted the events of the meeting, Jorge looked confused.

Finally, when Carlos paused, Jorge asked, "Why would you agree to something so dangerous? I know you two were friends, but why jeopardize everything you've built?" Jorge was not accustomed to questioning his longtime boss and idol. Carlos made the decisions, and Jorge carried out his orders, effectively and ruthlessly. But this just didn't make sense to him.

Carlos was obviously frustrated, having to explain himself to his bodyguard, but Jorge was more than that. They had been through so much together. It would take two hands to count the number of times Jorge had saved Carlos's life.

"There are many reasons why I am willing to help Will Hawkins. First, he is a friend, and you more than anyone should understand that I am, by nature, a very loyal person. I give friendship out freely, and I demand it in return. Second, Will Hawkins saved my life in London one night many years ago. I truly believe I wouldn't be here today if he had not intervened on my behalf. Third, because the favor Will has asked from me is beyond the scope of loyalty and a fight that happened so long ago, he has agreed, in principle, to insert one of our key people into the Drug Enforcement Council. I believe that could be very beneficial as we plan our shipment schedule and US points of entry."

Jorge broke into a big grin. "The picture is getting clearer, jefe."

"And finally," Carlos continued, "once the accidents have been executed and Will Hawkins is the president of the United States, I will have leverage over the most powerful man in the world." The way Carlos stated his final point sent chills down Jorge's spine. Jorge had killed more people than he could count, but at that moment, he was reminded that Carlos Pendrill had the power and the cojones to be truly evil.

For the next two hours, Carlos and Jorge discussed the type of accidents that would be easiest to execute and that would generate the most US and world press coverage. As the discussion was winding down, Carlos took a moment to recap the discussion. "Okay, Jorge, over the next forty-eight hours you're going to research the viability of our ideas. We need to identify a nuclear power facility that is very rural, but near enough to a major airport so we can get in and get out before anyone realizes there was a possibility of foul play. Next, we need to identify a trucking company that hauls toxic waste on the US highway system. Once we know who's moving the stuff, we need to identify a common route that passes by a high-profile waterway. After that, you need to pinpoint the nerve-gas storage facilities. There are only a few, so choose a location that is most easily infiltrated while maximizing the distance from our other accidents. And finally, find me a hydroelectric dam whose failure will result in a minimal loss of life. I know it's unrealistic to think we can do it without killing anyone, but let's not have any small cities downstream, either. And Jorge . . . I need this information yesterday."

As Jorge left the room, Carlos smiled to himself. This was the first time he'd felt an adrenaline rush in a long time.

o o o

Fifteen hundred miles away in the office of the chairman at GenSquare, Bo Hawkins and John Rollins were discussing Will's campaign. Rollins finally decided that, while he had pledged his silence to Will, his true allegiance over the past twenty-five years had been with Bo, his largest and most powerful customer. Bo was lamenting the fact that the public opinion polls, while increasing in favorability toward his son, weren't rising fast enough to ensure Will's election.

"Bo, I believe Will has a plan that will accelerate his popularity," Rollins interrupted.

"Really, and what might that be?"

"Well, I'm not sure where to start, but I have to tell you: I promised Will I wouldn't share his plan with anyone."

Bo exploded. "I'm not anyone, goddammit, I'm his father! Not to mention your friend and meal ticket over the past twenty-five years."

"I'm very clear on that, Bo. That's why I'm here now." Rollins proceeded to explain the entire environmental sabotage plan to Bo Hawkins. When he was finished, a deafening silence followed.

Then, Bo leaned forward and said in a voice as quiet as a snake's hiss, "What in the hell do you think you're doing? You're actually going to condone a front-running candidate for US president interacting with a known, big-time drug smuggler so they can win the sympathy of the American public? You must be out of your fucking mind."

Rollins took a deep breath and raised his hands in an appeasing motion. "Actually, Bo, I believe it's a brilliant plan. No one in the press has ever figured out that Will and Carlos Pendrill were college room-mates in London. The accidents themselves are not intended to injure or kill, but rather to catch the attention of the press and the American people. The David Ellis alliance is beyond reproach. In fact, Ellis's popularity currently exceeds that of both Will and President Hughes. And finally, with all the risks that are associated with a plan of this type, I believe it is infinitely safer than the plan you and I discussed a few weeks ago."

Again, there was silence as Bo contemplated his adviser's point of view. Finally, Bo agreed to keep quiet and let his son execute the plan that he was supposed to have no knowledge of. After John Rollins left his office, Bo sat quietly, considering what he had just heard. While the plan was dangerous, it had merit. But he decided he would also keep his own clandestine plan in play . . . for insurance.

# eighteen

Forty-eight hours later, Carlos Pendrill and Jorge Castilla reconvened at the Pendrill compound to review the accident plan. As usual, Carlos was quite impressed with Jorge's resourcefulness and efficiency. In just two days, Jorge had assembled the team, identified the accident locations, and outlined the methods by which the accidents would be executed.

Jorge explained, "The accidents will be geographically dispersed to minimize the chance of anyone making a connection from one to the other. The accident team will enter the US at a high-volume border crossing to avoid detection. The accident sites are identified."

"All right, give me the topline on the accident specifics and locations."

"Let me give you the rundown in the order they'll be executed. First, Transcon is the transportation company that hauls the bulk of US toxic waste. I was surprised to find that more waste is moved via rail than truck, but we were still able to find a target. There's a mining operation in Utah that requires a variety of toxic chemicals to excavate a rare mineral. Transcon has the contract to remove the toxic wastes created in this process. The nearest toxic-waste dump is in New Mexico, so the waste trucks must take Interstate 70 east to Denver and Interstate 25 south to New Mexico. There is a stretch of eastbound I-70 called Glenwood Canyon. This canyon was carved by the Colorado River. A strategically placed smart bomb, detonated at the right moment, should send the truck off the highway, down a steep embankment, and right into the river. The damages will be minimal due to the high volume of water that flows through the canyon, but the press will eat it up."

Carlos smiled. "I like it. What's next?"

"A nuclear power facility in South Carolina. It's a very rural area. As it turns out, there is a disgruntled assistant director of the operation who has been widely quoted in the local press criticizing management's cost-cutting tactics that are jeopardizing safety and key employee retention. The plan is to compromise the assistant director and use money and a message to management as our leverage."

"What's your confidence level that this guy will play?"

"Well, the guy is divorced with two kids in college and an annual salary of $47,000. So the money will be tempting. His profile would also indicate that an incident that would gain press attention would support his strong criticisms of the safety precautions management has ignored in recent years."

"All right, how does it work?"

"It's really quite simple. Our guy plants a device equipped to deploy a highly concentrated form of acid that will quickly eat through metal. Once the acid reaches the cooling system of the reactor, water will be introduced to the molten core, starting a minor meltdown."

Carlos had a skeptical expression. "Won't the acid leave some indication that the reactor was tampered with?"

"Actually, no," Jorge quickly answered. "The minor explosion, along with the accompanying toxic steam, will eliminate the clues that would indicate any tampering took place."

"Two down, two to go," Carlos said, smiling. "I'm intrigued."

"Nerve gas. We've identified a facility in Nebraska that is currently working with a new strain of sarin gas that will be the deadliest ever. The kicker is, the only way this gas can generate its deadly compounds is to be introduced to an outside force—for example, being dropped out of a plane or launched by a mortar. Our plan is to create this force by toppling a large storage tank in the laboratory, already having attached a tiny vial of the sarin to the outside to ensure contact and the resulting release of the deadly gas. We're still working on the appropriate insider to help us, but we've got three or four weeks until the execution of accident number three."

"Sounds viable for now, but I will want an update prior to execution."

"Got it."

"And finally?"

"The grand finale: the Woodrow Wilson hydroelectric dam on the Columbia River in Washington state. We're certain that a structural failure at this location will minimize loss of life while creating a huge media event. The hundred-foot wall of water will carve a path of destruction that will make a tidal wave look like a ripple on a pond. But the beauty is that the water will not interact with any significant population centers, except a few hard-core outsiders in their cabins, for about 150 miles. By then the wall of water will have subsided, and flooding of the magnitude of Vermont after Hurricane Irene would be the result. We've got structural engineers working on the best way to create a failure of this type, but they've assured me it's very doable."

"Jorge, once again, I applaud your efforts. I believe these accidents should achieve the desired effect, and our US friends will generate the groundswell of support necessary to propel their candidate into the Oval Office. Now, before you are completely engulfed by the next stages of your elaborate plans, let's celebrate."

With that, the two men adjourned to the south wing of Pendrill's estate where Mexico City's "beautiful people" were assembled to drink and dance the night away. When Carlos and Jorge entered the huge, Spanish-style ballroom, four dark-haired, dark-skinned Latin beauties approached. The men took a lady on each arm and walked toward the bar, smiling. Carlos considered the benefits of power in Mexico exquisite. He couldn't wait for the exponential power surge associated with the Will Hawkins presidency that now seemed quite probable.

o o o

Will Hawkins, David Ellis, and Jack McCarthy met in the outer office of Will's Dallas office. Ellis had just been escorted to the forty-first floor by Stephanie Wood. After a brief greeting and some handshakes, Will opened the door to his office and escorted the others in. David Ellis was momentarily stunned. This was not the type of setting in which his meetings with politicians usually took place.

Will Hawkins sensed Ellis's hesitation and asked, "Is there anything wrong, David?"

"Not at all, Will. I'm just not accustomed to political meetings in Shangri-La."

The three men laughed as Will motioned them to the couch and chairs at the far end of the office. Once settled, the men's conversation almost immediately took on a more serious tone.

Will launched into the discussion by stating, "David, I am honored that you would take time out of your busy schedule to fly to Dallas and meet with us. So, in an effort to minimize your time away from the foundation's important agenda, I would like to share with you my vision for the future of America and the reasons why I believe our alliance makes so much sense."

David nodded affirmatively but thought to himself that Will Hawkins was playing him for a fool. Does he actually think I don't know what he's going to say? Hell, he practically stole his script from my organization!

Will began pontificating, which made Jack nervous. Will had refused Jack's talk sheet for the meeting, telling Jack that he was very comfortable interacting with the likes of David Ellis without the benefit of preparation. Will spent the next fifteen minutes discussing his platforms. He covered taxes, the economy, healthcare, crime, and foreign policy. When Will paused, waiting for David Ellis's reaction, Jack decided to interject some key omissions, namely the environment and drugs. But before a word had exited his lips, David Ellis spoke.

"Senator, your platforms are sound. But you have chosen to ignore one of the foundation's primary reasons for existing: the environment."

Jack cringed, and Will reacted as if he'd been slapped in the face. How could he have forgotten David Ellis's favorite topic and the very agenda item on which he had risked everything? Will shot a look at Jack, implicating him in the omission, but was quick to realize that the look of disgust on Jack's face was directly related to his unwillingness to spend more time preparing for this meeting.

Will sensed the ball was in his court and immediately countered with an expression of pure innocence and transparency. "I was saving the best for last, David."

Ellis seemed to accept this, though everyone in the room knew it was bullshit. Will continued, "I am appalled at the Hughes administration's complete lack of effort concerning America's environment. They have let big business and industry write their own rules, and our children's future is in jeopardy. The environment is my passion, and I will diligently put legislation in place that will manage and ultimately eliminate big business's ability to put profits ahead of our country's future."

Jack smiled inwardly. Although Will had obviously forgotten this important agenda item, he had recovered with passion and conviction. David Ellis had to know that Will Hawkins could deliver the goods to the American people.

Ellis spoke first. "Senator, I like your style. You and I agree more than we disagree, and I believe in your stance on the environment . . . whether you actually believe it or not."

Will made as if to respond, but Ellis held up his hand for silence and continued. "Based on our previous discussions as well as today's meeting, I am ready to announce the foundation's full support of your candidacy—based on one condition."

Will and Jack leaned forward.

"I would like you to make me secretary of the interior. That way, I can continue to focus on the environmental issues confronting our country today, while you focus on all the other issues that face a twenty-first-century American president."

The time it took for Will Hawkins to respond to the proposed deal was actually less than fifteen seconds, but it seemed like an eternity to Jack. When Will did say something, it was lacking the usual eloquence the senator from Texas was known for. "You've got yourself a deal, Mr. Ellis."

Will Hawkins's office was electrified with excitement. Will and David excitedly shook hands, and Will simultaneously put an arm around Jack. But the only thing on Jack's mind was, "one down and one to go." The next step in the campaign was to increase Will Hawkins's focus on the war against drugs.

# nineteen

Jack McCarthy was patiently waiting in Will Hawkins's outer office for his early evening appointment. On the Hawkins campaign, early evening was defined as 8:00 to 10:00 p.m. Jack was sitting in one of the soft, leather waiting room chairs absentmindedly watching Stephanie Wood gather her things.

"Jack, did you hear a word I said?" Stephanie asked.

"I'm sorry, Stephanie. I was thinking about something else. What'd you say?"

She gave him an exasperated look. "I was saying that Mr. Hawkins kept me late this evening, and I missed meeting a friend for dinner. I was just wondering if, after your meeting, you wanted to go out and get a bite to eat. I was thinking maybe Javier's."

Jack had done a good job to date of avoiding any interaction with Stephanie outside of the workplace. But he also knew that since she seemed to be attracted to him, he had easier access to Will Hawkins. She made it very difficult for the people who treated her disrespectfully or those whom she didn't like to get on the candidate's calendar. So Jack responded, "That sounds great, Stephanie, but I'm not sure how long this meeting is going to last."

Stephanie appeared surprised but quickly regrouped. "That's okay, Jack. I'll get our name on the list and wait in the bar until you get there. I could actually use a large margarita."

They both laughed as Stephanie's hotline, the number Will Hawkins gave only to key individuals, began to ring. When Stephanie realized which line was ringing, she got very serious very quickly. Jack noticed the immediate change in her demeanor.

"Will Hawkins's office, may I help you?"

The caller was Carl Peterson, the alias Will Hawkins and Carlos Pendrill had agreed upon for any calls Carlos would have to make to the candidate. Stephanie knew that any call from someone on the hotline list was to be treated extremely confidentially. Her normal routine was to ensure the line was on scramble and to be sure Hawkins's door was closed. But at that moment, she looked at Jack, who was staring at her intently, and her mind wandered to what the evening might have in store.

She continued, "He's currently on another line, Mr. Peterson, but I will let him know you are on hold."

She quickly scribbled a note and entered Hawkins's office to make him aware of the important caller. When she returned, she hurried directly back to her phone, leaving the office door open slightly, obviously in a rush to transfer the call from Mr. Peterson.

As soon as she transferred the call, she looked at Jack and smiled. "Mr. Hawkins said this call should take only a few minutes, and then he'll be ready to see you. I'm going to go ahead and take off to get our name on the list. Thursday nights in Dallas can be a nightmare."

"Sounds great," Jack said, wondering who Mr. Peterson was. "I'll see you there in an hour or so."

Stephanie was obviously excited and bounced out of the office, having completely forgotten to scramble the important call—or close the senator's office door.

o o o

"Carlos," Will Hawkins answered in an uncertain tone, "I'm surprised to hear from you so soon."

"I'm a man of action, Will," Carlos said, laughing. "You requested an update once the plans were laid out, and I'm also a man of my word."

The two men discussed the process Pendrill's team had gone through to identify key accident sites while eliminating the possibility of significant loss of life. Will Hawkins was getting more and more nervous. He was wondering, once again, how he had gotten himself into a situation like this. But this is my plan. And it will get me into the White House.

Carlos began to explain the specifics surrounding the accidents: the toxic-waste truck that would plunge into the Colorado River, a nuclear power plant melting down in the rural midsection of South Carolina . . . Will interrupted Carlos, wanting to better understand the details of how the accidents would be achieved and especially the potential loss of life that would accompany them.

"Will, I am a perfectionist. I always achieve my objectives effectively and efficiently. I don't have time to explain all the details that my team has spent countless hours perfecting. If you don't trust our capabilities, maybe we should stop now."

"No, I . . . I trust your judgment. It's just that . . . Never mind, what else do you have?"

Carlos laid out the plan for replicating a nerve gas leak in a Nebraska facility. The accident would closely coincide with a House subcommittee report on the proliferation of biological weapons worldwide. It was Will's turn to smile to himself. He had to admit; that was a nice touch.

Then Carlos outlined the final event, the structural collapse of a hydroelectric dam on the Columbia River in Washington.

Will was stunned. The thought of the destructive power of an accident of this type left him speechless. A small voice deep in his mind said that this was too much. When he regained his composure, he lashed out at Carlos. "This is unacceptable! The devastation and carnage associated with an accident of this type is way beyond what is necessary."

Carlos responded aggressively. "No, Will, what's unacceptable is your inability to grasp the fact that your plan is not without its downsides.

Property will be damaged. People will be killed. If you don't have the stomach for it, then walk away. Presidents have the guts to make the tough calls. I'm beginning to wonder if you have that ability."

From the silence on the line, Carlos thought once again that he had Will right where he wanted him. Then, without warning, Will exploded.

"Who the fuck do you think you are, talking to me that way? I have the resolve to make any decision necessary!"

o o o

From the waiting area outside, Jack could hear Hawkins screaming into the telephone. His first reaction was to tune out the conversation, assuming it was none of his business. But as the yelling continued, Jack became concerned. He stood and walked to the doorway, but he couldn't see Will, around the corner at his desk. Jack considered walking in to see if everything was all right but then decided against it. Still, his concern increased as Will's yelling did.

Jack could not decide what to do. Should he go back to his office and wait for Will to call? Should he enter Will's office and ask if he needed anything? He quickly decided that neither of those options were professionally appealing, but he couldn't stop wondering what was agitating Will Hawkins to a degree he had never experienced from the candidate.

Then Jack eyed Stephanie Wood's phone console. Jack slowly approached the assistant's desk the way he might approach a dangerous animal. He studied the console, rationalizing to himself that it was his lifelong "curiosity affliction" that was drawing him to listen in on the front-running Democratic candidate for president of the United States.

When Jack lifted the receiver of Will Hawkins's confidential line, he was actually surprised to hear voices; one he clearly recognized as Will Hawkins, and the other was obviously the voice of the mysterious caller, Carl Peterson. Will shifted his attention to the content of the conversation.

The slightly accented voice of Peterson was saying, "Will, you have to calm down. All I am saying is that you can't expect me to execute catastrophic environmental disasters on your behalf and not be willing to accept the fact that some loss of life is both necessary and acceptable."

Jack could not believe what he was hearing. His heart had begun to beat so loudly, he was sure it could be heard through the phone. His first instinct was to hang up the phone and run. What little he had heard was incomprehensible, but he was also mesmerized by the conversation he was eavesdropping on.

Will Hawkins was responding to his caller's comments. "When I originally developed the plan to pull in The Future State Foundation, it was conceptual in nature, but this . . . I can accept the moderate number of deaths that will coincide with the toxic-waste spill, the reactor meltdown, and the nerve gas accident. But I am very concerned about the structural failure of a dam that size. The destruction and loss of life associated with that specific plan concerns me greatly. I too am a man of action, but I am not a mass murderer."

"And Carlos Pendrill is not a political lackey," the caller shouted. "You came to me asking a significant favor. I have gone to great lengths to accommodate."

They were still talking, but Jack was no longer listening. He was numb. He had just overheard his boss, a front-runner for the presidency of the United States, making a deal with one of the world's largest drug dealers to implement a plan that equated to environmental Armageddon.

Jack quietly hung up the phone and left Stephanie Wood's waiting area. His mind was spinning, and he was experiencing the full gamut of emotions: Anger, fear, loneliness, and disbelief were combining to create a feeling of utter confusion. Jack rode the elevator to the parking garage in a daze, but still pulled it together and phoned Stephanie to cancel on dinner.

o o o

At the same time, Will and Carlos were agreeing to move forward with their plans and to revisit the dam discussion later. Once Will had hung up, he took a moment to compose himself and then strode to his office door to receive Jack McCarthy. What he saw nearly made his heart stop. His office door was slightly ajar, against his strict instructions. His heart pounded as he approached the door. How would he explain his outbursts to Jack? As he opened the door, he was relieved to see that no one was in the waiting area. His thoughts quickly shifted to the firm "teaching moment" he would have with Stephanie regarding the strict confidentiality that certain phone calls must be afforded.

# twenty

Jack McCarthy was driving around Dallas in a daze. The information he had just been exposed to was beyond his comprehension. A US senator, one of the richest men in the country and a man who had a legitimate shot at the next presidency, was plotting with one of the world's most ruthless drug cartel leaders to create an environmental holocaust.

"This cannot be happening," Jack said out loud. But it was, and he had no idea what to do or whom to turn to. He'd been driving around for an hour with no conscious plan. He suddenly realized that he was at Winfrey Point on the east side of White Rock Lake. The parklike setting was somehow soothing to his inner turmoil, so he got out of his car and walked toward the lake. It was a beautiful night in Dallas, and the reflection of a distant downtown skyline reflected off the water.

How could he have gotten into such a mess? His thoughts strayed. If only I hadn't picked up the phone, I'd still be happily working on a presidential campaign, naïvely lobbying for an American hero to take over the Oval Office. Instead, I feel as if I'm standing on the edge of a great abyss.

Taking the next step was necessary, but where that step led was without definition. Obviously, Will Hawkins would go to unimagined lengths to get what he wanted. The question was, if he found out that

Jack had overheard his plan, what would he do and how would Jack respond? Legitimate questions that lacked concrete answers.

After fifteen more minutes of contemplation, anger, denial, and ultimately, resolve, Jack decided to go home. As he pulled into his driveway, he realized that Carrie was there. He took a deep breath and tried to compose himself. This was clearly something he could not share with her right now, regardless of how close they had become. When he entered the kitchen from the garage, Carrie immediately knew something was wrong.

"You look horrible. What happened to you today?"

"Just a bitch of a day on the campaign trail," Jack responded. "This campaign shit makes the agency business look like a walk in the park." He attempted to smile.

Carrie laughed and took him by the hand into the living room. "You sit right here and let me get you a big, fat scotch."

"That's the best offer I've had all day," Jack said.

"And that's only the beginning of what I have to offer," Carrie replied in her best husky voice. She returned with the scotch and tried to initiate conversation. But every attempt she made was met with silence, and Jack staring off into space.

She was clearly getting frustrated with the situation when Jack finally caught on and said, "Honey, I'm sorry. I just can't clear my head of all the details. Let's start again."

With that, Carrie straddled his lap, grabbed his face, and gave him a long, passionate kiss. "As you can tell, I'm totally committed to clearing your mind of all the details," she said, laughing.

"And you're doing a damn good job of it," Jack said as he stood and led her toward the bedroom.

The next morning, Jack woke slowly, realizing it was very light in the room. He turned to kiss Carrie and realized she was gone. He looked at the clock. It was 8:07.

"Shit!" He hadn't slept past 6:00 in months. The last thing he wanted at the campaign office was for others to sense something was different or wrong. As he lay there willing himself out of bed, Jack thought that while he had slept a solid nine hours, the bulk of his sleep was filled with dreams of a sinister candidate and the terrible things he was doing to get elected.

What could he do? Whom could he talk to? Involving others was dangerous—to him and to them. But he didn't feel capable of going it alone. He needed a confidant: someone he could bounce things off of someone who could help him figure out how to address the situation quietly but ultimately put a halt to the planned atrocities.

There was really only one answer: Steve Bess. Over the past several months, Steve had become his mentor, adviser, and a very close friend. Obviously, Steve was in the dark, just as he was. There was no way a man of Steve's integrity would ever be party to something this outrageous. But it was dangerous. The last thing Jack wanted was for anyone close to him to get hurt because he'd listened in on that psychopathic conversation. But counter to that feeling was the thought of innocent people being hurt or killed because he was unwilling or unable to make the tough call.

At that very moment, Jack knew in his heart he had to stop them. He also knew he couldn't do it alone. He would tell Steve Bess everything he knew, and together they would find a way to do the right thing.

o o o

While Jack was agonizing over his predicament in Dallas, Sgt. Maj. Ian McKay was meeting with his superior and friend, Col. Charles Cavanaugh.

Cavanaugh said, "I don't understand, Ian. You're in as good shape as you were twenty years ago, and I know you love your job."

"I did love my job, Charles. I just don't have the same fire in the belly that I used to. Training these guys so that they can risk their lives on a regular basis is starting to get to me. The last thing I want to do is get soft in my old age and be responsible for one or more of these kids not coming home." Ian was lying; he actually felt sick when he thought of someone else training his boys.

"Ian, is there anything I can say or do that would change your mind?" Charles pleaded.

"I'm afraid not, Charles. I've made up my mind, and I know it's the right decision."

"Well then, Major McKay," Cavanaugh said in a booming voice, "I will support your decision."

As Cavanaugh stood, he snapped off a formal salute and then hugged McKay as a father would a son. When he stepped back, Ian noticed the moisture in Cavanaugh's eyes. It was enough to almost send him over the edge. Ian saluted back and left without saying another word.

When McKay returned home, his sharp mind had erased the emotional moment felt only twenty minutes earlier, and he was ready to go to work. His plan was extremely well thought out but not without its risks. The first step was to finalize his false documents: passport, UK driver's license, and credit cards. Once he had established a new identity, it would be time to travel to the US. Once there, he would go to Dallas and begin monitoring Sen. Will Hawkins's every move. What was his daily schedule? What was his travel schedule? How did the senator's security detail work? What were their schedules? Did they have tendencies that offered openings?

Ian knew that he had to treat the surveillance as if he were planning to assassinate the candidate. He needed to get close enough to Hawkins to slip him a note without any of the security detail noticing. The best option would be in a crowded area: walking on a busy street, strolling through a crowded airport. Or—he couldn't believe he hadn't thought of it sooner—at a campaign rally or speech. American politicians loved to grip-and-grin with their supporters. It was perfect.

Then, once Hawkins was aware of the problems Ian could cause in his race to the presidency, Ian would contact him with the offer: his silence in exchange for $25 million cash. Not a massive dent in the Hawkins family fortune but still extremely difficult for the senator to find and hide in a short amount of time. Once the offer was agreed to,

Ian would arrange a meeting to make the exchange, and then he would disappear. The money would give Lizzie the life she deserved, and Will Hawkins would spend the rest of his life wondering if he would ever be publicly accused of murdering a British soldier so long ago.

# twenty-one

reg Larson sat in the conference room at *The Dallas Free Press* lamenting the fact that he still hadn't had a major breakthrough on the Hawkins series. He silently waited to meet his newly assigned researcher. The last one had been more interested in smoking dope than uncovering big news. Larson was kicking himself for even taking the campaign assignment.

His frustration hit an all-time high the moment John Sterling, his new researcher, entered the room. Sterling was a tall, lanky man with a ponytail, multiple earrings, and a Coors Light T-shirt that had probably been new when Clinton was in office. Larson's reaction was immediate. "Shit, I need a researcher, and they send me another Olympic bonging champion."

Sterling's response was just as quick. "Fuck you, Mr. Prima Donna. I always heard you were an arrogant prick, and now I know it for myself. What if I just take my pot-smoking, computer science PhD back through the door and leave your ass wondering how you'll ever find a meaningful story on our illustrious senator from Highland Park."

As Sterling turned toward the door he had just entered, Larson spoke. "Hey man, I'm sorry, that wasn't fair of me to say."

Sterling stopped, turned, and smiled. "I actually wasn't going to walk. Chambers would have had my ass. But I appreciate the apology anyway."

Larson laughed, "You know Chambers?"

"Yeah, I've been working on projects for him for years. He tells people I'm the best researcher he's ever known. Truth is, I'm the only one that will put up with his shit."

Larson laughed again. "You know, I think you and I are going to get along just fine. Now if you don't mind, we need to get to work."

The two men spent the next forty-five minutes discussing story angles that had not been previously covered. Larson said, "Let's go deep. I want to talk to his friends from grade school. I want to meet his first girlfriend. I want to know if he ever cheated on an exam. I want to know if he fucking inhaled."

Sterling nodded in agreement. "There has to be something on this guy. Nobody can be this clean. And if there is something there, I'm just the guy to find it."

"Good," Larson stated emphatically. "Get to work and see what you can find. Let's meet in a couple of days, and we'll see what you've come up with."

"I'm on it."

The two men shook hands as the researcher reassured Larson that he would find something.

After Sterling left, Larson remained in the conference room contemplating this highly frustrating situation. He had accepted this assignment believing that he could generate a meaningful story, regardless of what others at the paper believed. This was his chance to regain the limelight. His name had been out of the journalistic upper echelon for quite some time, and he needed a breakthrough. He knew he couldn't live on his investigative reputation indefinitely. This was a business of results, and he knew in his heart there was something in Will Hawkins's past that he could leverage. And once he had it firmly in his grasp, he would request and get a one-on-one interview with Will Hawkins that would change the face of American politics for the new millennium.

Larson rationalized to himself that his mission involved more than just personal reward. He had never respected Will Hawkins for his politics. Hawkins, in his mind, had gotten to where he was today because of money, and that's not what the Founding Fathers intended. Being president of the United States was supposed to be about leadership, ideas, and the people, not money and power. Larson realized that there had to be a better candidate out there. That's why he was determined to rain on the Hawkins parade.

○ ○ ○

Jack McCarthy and Steve Bess shook hands inside the front door of Bob's Steakhouse, a longtime Dallas eatery. After a short wait at the crowded bar surrounded by a throng of Dallas's elite, they were led to their out-of-the-way table for two.

The small talk continued for another five minutes until Steve said, "Jack, what's up? When you invited me to dinner, it sounded important."

"It is, Steve. I'm not sure where to start, but I stumbled on some information regarding the campaign, and I'm not sure what to do next."

Jack proceeded to recap the entire portion of the conversation he had overheard: the call from Carlos Pendrill; the plan to execute a series of environmental accidents that would taint the current administration and solidify the alliance with David Ellis's foundation. When Jack had finished his five-minute overview of what he had heard, Steve Bess was silent. It was as if the life had been extracted from his rigid body. When he finally did regain some composure, his reaction was grounded in doubt.

"Jack, do you know what you're saying? Are you absolutely sure of what you heard?" Jack remained silent, but his eyes bored in on Bess, reaffirming the validity of his story.

"Holy shit," Bess said, shaking his head in shock. "This is the type of information that could create worldwide instability. The political system that much of the world admires and desires, gone in the wink of an eye. Jesus, what in the hell does he think he's doing? He has to be stopped."

"I agree," Jack said, "but we've got to remain calm and take control of the situation. That's why I called you. So do me a favor and provide that calming influence I was expecting from you."

Steve took a deep breath, hoping to clear his head. "You're right. Nothing has happened yet. We just need to intervene before anything does. Got any thoughts?"

"Well, as a matter of fact, I do. But to be honest, none of them are very appealing."

"Run them by me. We've got to start somewhere."

"Well, my first thought was to go to the president, but," Jack started to laugh, "I have a feeling my word against Will Hawkins's would leave something to be desired."

"I agree; we'd both be labeled crackpots before we could ever get out of the Oval Office. That is, if we could even get in."

Jack continued, "My next thought was to approach the chairman of the Democratic National Committee, but I'm sure we'd meet the same resistance."

"I agree," Bess added quickly.

"So then I thought maybe an approach that was closer to home was in order."

"And?" Bess added, questioning.

"I thought about Bo Hawkins. The stakes are awfully high for him to ignore this type of information."

"Again, I agree, but we're talking about his son here. I think his first reaction will be to defend him."

"Which leads us to John Rollins," Jack said. "He's the logical choice. He's our boss, and he has the credibility to approach Bo Hawkins and put a stop to this madness."

Steve Bess interjected, "You're right. He may be a madman on the job, but he's an ethical guy. I've worked with him for fifteen years, and the one thing I would trust him to do is the right thing."

Jack and Steve continued the discussion for another forty-five minutes. They strategized every angle, determining the best way to approach Rollins. When they had exhausted their discussion of every possible reaction they might encounter, they agreed that Steve would approach Rollins the following day in an effort to maximize reaction time to the events that were most assuredly under way. Steve left the restaurant, and Jack paid the bill.

As Jack drove home, he felt as if a weight had been lifted from his shoulders. Sharing his problems with someone else had been a truly cathartic experience. But he wasn't ready to share this information with Carrie. It was too dangerous, so he was actually relieved when he pulled into his driveway and realized she wasn't there.

# twenty-two

Sgt. Major Ian McKay was having dinner with his niece, Lizzie, and her mother, Patricia. McKay was dreading the interrogation that would ensue when he told them he was leaving the service. So instead of addressing the situation head-on, he had taken them to a trendy restaurant, a place well beyond any of their means, for a celebration.

After more than an hour of small talk, while Ian consistently encouraged both women to "drink up," Patricia finally said, "Ian, we've waited patiently all evening for you to tell us what's going on. Now what's this celebration all about?"

Ian fidgeted nervously. "Great news, girls: I've decided to leave the service. I've had enough. So, I'm packing it in and following my dream to see the world."

The reaction was just what he had suspected: stunned silence mixed with looks of shock, sadness, and disbelief. Lizzie was the first to regain her composure. "But Uncle Ian, I thought you loved your job. In fact, just last year you told me you'd die a British soldier. What happened?"

Patricia added, "And what do you mean 'following your dream to see the world'? You've always said the only good reason to leave England was to fight a war. My God, I don't know what to say."

Ian feigned a mixture of anger and frustration and said, "I thought my two favorite women in the world would be happy for me. This is supposed to be a celebration."

Patricia, believing she'd hurt Ian's feelings, quickly retreated. "It's just that you caught us by surprise. If this is what makes you happy, then by all means, let's celebrate." Patricia raised her glass and toasted, "To Ian McKay, the best pseudo brother-in-law, uncle, and friend a girl could ever have."

The three raised their glasses in a silent toast, and Lizzie asked excitedly, "If you're going to see the world, where are you going first?"

"Well, believe it or not, my first adventure is to America. I've been planning my itinerary for a while, and I actually leave the day after tomorrow."

Again, the two were shocked by the news of the nearly immediate departure.

"Jesus, Ian!" Patricia blurted out. "How long have you been planning this? I'm starting to feel like you're hiding something from us."

Ian was caught by surprise, but he quickly recovered and explained, "I haven't been hiding anything. I broke the news to Charles last week, and I called to set up this dinner with you two the next day. I'm just ready for the next chapter in my life, and now is as good a time as any to start."

Lizzie eagerly broke in. "Well, tell us about your plans. Where are you going? How long are you going to be gone?"

So Ian began the explanation of his journey. Flying to New York, where he would stay for a few days, he would then catch a train to Washington, DC, where he would stay a week and soak in every historical attraction the city had to offer. Then on to Dallas.

Patricia asked, "What's in Dallas?"

"Well, I've always been intrigued by the Kennedy assassination. And if I'm touring America, Texas is one of a handful of states that I want to be able to say I've been to. And . . ." Ian was struggling to come up with any other good reasons why he would be visiting Dallas, but Patricia broke in and saved the day.

"And," she said smiling, "you obviously know a woman there."

Relieved, Ian lied, "You got me."

And before it was necessary to continue, Lizzie interrupted, "Isn't Dallas where that presidential candidate Will Hawkins is from?"

Ian's heart raced, but his exterior remained unfazed. He was about to respond when Lizzie continued, "I think he is so impressive. And so good-looking."

Ian's emotions got the better of him. "He is not impressive. He is scum. He's just another rich politician using his money to buy power. He is everything that is wrong with democracy in this world."

Ian's outburst caught the two women by surprise. They had never known him to be so emotionally involved in politics.

Lizzie spoke first. "I'm sorry, Uncle Ian. I was just making conversation. I really don't know that much about him."

Ian relaxed. "No, honey, I'm sorry. My political viewpoints aren't appropriate at a dinner with you two, celebrating the biggest life change I'll ever experience. I shouldn't have overreacted."

"Enough said," Lizzie responded.

As the three finished dinner, Patricia and Ian exchanged glances, both knowing that the other was fully aware there was more to this situation than the surface conversation had indicated.

o o o

Greg Larson and John Sterling had planned on meeting at the Greenville Avenue Bar and Grill at 9:00 p.m. Larson arrived early and was sitting at the long, half-empty bar when Sterling entered. Larson's reaction to Sterling's appearance was similar to their first meeting. But this time Larson refrained from any sarcastic comments, remembering that Sterling was no pushover.

The two men shook hands, and Larson asked, "Did you find anything?"

"Patience, my man, first things first," Sterling responded while signaling the barkeep to bring him a beer.

After what seemed like an eternity to Larson, the beer arrived, and Sterling turned toward him on his barstool. "I think I've got something you're going to be very interested in."

"Go on."

"After our last conversation, I realized that the bulk of our Hawkins research has focused on his life in the US. So I chose to immediately investigate his years at Oxford. It actually wasn't at all difficult to identify when he was there and then find someone else who was there at the same time. Once I found someone, I introduced myself as a government representative conducting an official candidate background check."

"There is no such thing."

"I know that and you know that, but Barbara Pollock from Leeds, UK, doesn't."

Larson smiled. "I'm beginning to like your style. Go on."

"Anyway, Ms. Pollock had an Oxford yearbook and was actually quite helpful. First, there's a picture in the yearbook of the Debate Society. And guess who's standing next to Senator Will Hawkins in the picture?" Sterling paused for effect. "Carlos Pendrill and Will Hawkins were in the Debate Society together."

"That's very interesting, John, but that doesn't mean—"

"Hold on, man, it gets better."

Sterling then proceeded to tell Larson that not only were Hawkins and Pendrill in the Society together, but they had also been good friends . . . and roommates.

Larson could not suppress his excitement. "You mean to tell me that our future president and the biggest drug dealer in the free world were friends and roommates in graduate school? This is too fucking good for words. You've got to get me more. Have they kept in touch? When was the last time Pendrill was in the US? Where was Hawkins during that time? I need everything, John."

"I'm looking, but there's no guarantee I'll find anything."

Larson leaned back in his stool and said, "Whether or not you find anything more, I'm going to rock Will Hawkins's world." With that, both men hoisted their glasses in a silent toast.

# twenty-three

As the car carrying the four Mexican nationals approached the US-Mexico border in Juarez, the vehicle looked like all the others waiting in the daily traffic jam at the busy border crossing. Despite the vehicle's normal appearance, however, it was actually quite different. The run-down 2003 Ford Taurus was really a mobile arsenal with enough weapons to rival even the most sophisticated military vehicle. The four passengers had been specially trained by an ex-US Marine who had gotten tired of his underpaid existence and signed on with Carlos Pendrill, who was willing to pay handsomely. The three men and one woman were the first team deployed by Jorge Castilla to begin the campaign of destruction engineered by Will Hawkins and Carlos Pendrill.

The group's mission was to shuttle all the necessary materials to Denver, Colorado, for redeployment to each of the four planned accident sites. Once the materials were disseminated, this group would carry out the first accident planned for Glenwood Canyon, a location two-and-a-half hours west of Denver.

As the car inched toward the border in the bumper-to-bumper traffic queue, the group was silent. Each of them focused on the vehicle itself: the automatic weapons stored within the specially made door panels; the plastic explosives that were expertly hidden in the spare tire; the acidic mixture stored in a specially lined aerosol can; the smart bombs hidden within the shells of two twenty-year-old boom boxes; and a variety of weapons such as hand grenades and pistols tucked into every nook and cranny the old Ford had to offer. Those were the thoughts of the car's passengers.

When the vehicle finally reached the customs checkpoint, an average-looking American approached the car. He appeared tired and uninterested in his daily duties.

"Hello," he said blandly, "may I see your papers, please?"

The four reached for their respective visas, knowing that their authenticity was beyond question. The border guard took each set of papers and eyed them carefully. While his commitment to his job was questionable, he was also highly skilled at spotting phony entry documents. However, after careful inspection, the guard was satisfied.

"Everything appears to be in order. Where are you headed?" he asked, already anticipating the cold beer awaiting him when he got off work in twenty-five minutes.

"To Denver," the driver answered in a thick accent, "to see family."

"Sounds good," the guard responded. "Please pull to the left. You are the lucky recipients of a random vehicle search."

Each of the passengers tensed at the request. While keeping their reaction concealed from the guard, two of the passengers appeared perceivably nervous to the group's leader in the front passenger seat. He slowly turned to the two in the back as the car eased to the search area. His look alone was enough to indicate that if either of them panicked, they would pay a price beyond any penalty the US Border Patrol could impose.

As the guard lazily approached, the driver exited his side of the car. The guard requested that the remainder of the passengers also get out and asked for the trunk to be opened. All four stood silently, barely moving, as the guard gave the car a cursory once-over. He was obviously not expecting to find anything, and his lackadaisical effort ensured that he wouldn't.

After less than two minutes, the guard turned to the group and said, "You're good to go. Enjoy your visit to the good old U S of A."

The four returned to their vehicle and drove across the bridge into El Paso, Texas. A minor hurdle, the first barrier to one of the largest terrorist attacks in the US, had just been cleared . . . easily.

o o o

Jack McCarthy and Steve Bess had agreed to meet at the Blue Goose for drinks and dinner around 6:00. As usual, the Lower Greenville eatery was filled with young professionals and college students ready to enjoy a libation and some of the best Mexican food in town. Jack arrived first. He grabbed a Coors Light out of the beer trough and worked his way to the bar to pay. Just as he squeezed to the front, he spotted Bess entering the restaurant and quickly flagged him down.

Bess looked tired, lacking the usual positive energy flowing from him that Jack had come to know and respect. The two men exchanged pleasantries and drank silently, waiting for their table. Fifteen minutes later, the young hostess, who could have easily been a model in a fashion magazine, sat them at a small table in the far corner of the dining area. They both nodded to one another, acknowledging that the out-of-the-way table in this very noisy restaurant was the perfect place to have the conversation they both had been dreading for two days.

Once seated, the two men quickly ordered more beer and the combination fajitas that would feed a large family.

Finally, Jack broke the silence. "What happened? Did Rollins throw you out of his office or just belittle you beyond the threshold of normal human anger?"

Bess laughed. "It was actually as quiet as you could possibly expect. I tried to get to the point as quickly as possible and stick to the facts."

"How did he take it?" Jack asked.

"Not good. First he turned white, like he'd seen the ghost of his mother. Finally, his color returned, but he never regained his composure.

He stammered and sat speechless for minutes at a time. He finally recovered enough to ask where I got my information. I explained how you had innocently stumbled on the plot. He was not happy with your method, but he seemed to understand your concern."

"So where did you net out? What's the next step?"

"Rollins asked me to let him sleep on it. He was in no condition to hatch a plan. He could barely get out a complete sentence," Bess said. "We agreed we would reconvene at 10:30 tomorrow morning. He needed a chance to digest what he had just heard, and the office is always empty on Saturday mornings. That'll give us the privacy we need to identify next steps."

The two men were all too eager to switch topics. They spent the rest of the dinner inventing small talk that would circumvent any conversation about the information that was so historically significant that neither of them could comprehend the magnitude. After numerous beers, the two men parted, agreeing to meet at the office on Saturday afternoon after Rollins and Bess had gotten back together to discuss their options. Jack and Steve stood, shook hands, and said goodbye before retreating to the private thoughts that neither of them could avoid.

# twenty-four

It was a beautiful morning in Dallas, a Saturday that Jack would have relished just weeks ago. Now, though, he felt as though the weight of the world was on his shoulders. As he lay awake in bed staring at Carrie, his thoughts wandered to the advisability of sharing his personal hell with her. It would be so much easier having someone to talk to. But he knew that wasn't a good idea. As much as he loved her, he couldn't be sure just how she might react. What if she believed it was best to go right to the authorities? He couldn't stop her. But he knew in his heart that would be the worst thing that could happen to this country and to them. So, problem solved. The best thing for Carrie was to not put her in a moral dilemma of that magnitude.

As if on cue, when Jack had decided in his own mind to not share his current problem with Carrie, he glanced at her and noticed she was staring at him.

"Where have you been?" she asked, smiling. "You were so far away just then, I don't think anyone could have reached you."

"Oh, I was just thinking about work. I've got so much shit to do," Jack nonchalantly responded.

"Well, let's do our best to keep your mind off of work for the next twenty minutes or so," Carrie said in a sultry whisper as she reached for him.

o o o

At that same moment, Steve Bess was entering the Texas Club for his weekly Saturday morning workout. Rain or shine, sickness, health, or hangover, Steve had been religiously working out at 8:30 Saturday mornings for more than ten years. As Bess entered the club, the desk attendant warmly greeted him.

"Morning, Mr. Bess. It's a great day to work out; it's empty in there."

"Thanks, Josh. I could use a good one," Bess responded, as he entered the locker room.

At nearly the same moment, the elevator door opened, and Josh found himself staring at an attractive blonde with the stereotypical big hair and the largest set of breasts he'd ever seen. Stretched on the T-shirt covering the woman's enormous chest was the word PowerSport.

"Hi," she said, "are you Joe?"

"No, Joe's not working today. Anything I can do for you?"

"Well," she continued, "I spoke with Joe earlier this week and was scheduled to sample PowerSport here today. It's a new sport and energy drink."

Josh hesitated. They were not supposed to admit solicitors without permission. "Wait a minute," he said. "Let me see if he left a note or anything."

"Sounds great," the blonde responded as she seductively walked over to a wall of photos.

Josh was in slow motion; he couldn't take his eyes off her body. Minutes later, when it was apparent he was not going to find a permission slip, he made an executive decision. He would let her in, regardless. What could it hurt to let a few middle-aged men view one of nature's incredible creations? Not to mention that he was hoping to get her number on the way out. "You know, I couldn't find a note from Joe authorizing your sampling, but . . . it's cool. Go on in."

"Thanks, Josh," the blonde said, reading his name tag. "I really appreciate your help." With that, she was buzzed into the women's locker room where she began to set up her sampling tray.

o o o

As Jack exited the bathroom, towel wrapped around his waist, Carrie was rummaging through his jeans, still on the floor next to his side of the bed.

"What are you looking for?" Jack asked.

"Your keys. I'm going to Café Brazil for some real coffee and take-out empanadas."

"Sounds awesome," Jack said sincerely. "I could use a little grease in the system."

Carrie smiled. "Drink a few beers with your new buddy Steve last night?"

"Just a few," Jack said, recalling more than just a few.

o o o

Steve Bess was struggling on the treadmill. His thoughts were currently focused on just how bad he was hurting. He used to be able to drink all night and work out the next morning without a bit of trouble. Now, he'd been on the treadmill for less than fifteen minutes and he felt nauseous. Just when he thought, fuck it, he spotted a female body coming his way that would stop a freight train. There was no way he was going to wimp out with the PowerSport girl anywhere near him.

"Hi," she said. "Would you like to try a sample of our new isotonic drink, PowerSport? It definitely helps during a tough workout."

"Well, at this point, I need all the help I can get," Steve responded.

The woman reached to her tray and handed Steve a sport bottle of the fruit-punch-flavored drink.

"This will do the trick when you're finished with your workout," she said, smiling. "How much longer are you going to go?"

"Probably about fifteen minutes," Steve responded, setting the drink in his treadmill cup holder.

Before he could think of anything else to say to this incredibly effective distraction, she smiled and moved on to the next customer. Steve watched her for the next few minutes, and then she was gone. The second half of the treadmill session was going much faster than the first.

o o o

Jack watched Carrie as she walked to his car in the driveway. He couldn't get over how close they'd become in the past few months. It made him feel guilty for not being able to confide in her. But as he watched this beautiful woman climb into his car, he knew there would be a right time to tell her his troubles; he just wasn't sure when that would be.

o o o

At the same moment, Steve Bess took a giant swig of his PowerSport sample.

o o o

Carrie turned the key in Jack's Saab. Instantly, the vehicle erupted in an explosion that rattled the gingerbread houses for two blocks around. Jack watched the surreal scene, not realizing that the window he was looking through no longer existed and that his face was covered in blood from the multiple glass fragments that had shot in his direction.

o o o

Steve Bess was suddenly feeling weak in the knees. He reached for a railing to steady himself and missed. He was dead before he hit the floor.

# twenty-five

Will Hawkins reclined in his office chair, feet on his desk, with his phone tucked under his chin. His usually confident demeanor was less apparent than normal. Carlos Pendrill was the recipient of this early afternoon call that provided some startling news. Will was a firm believer in always delivering a solution in conjunction with a problem. Therefore, he hadn't immediately made Carlos aware of the fact that Jack McCarthy had overheard the two of them discussing their accident plan. But now that the problem had been solved, it was easier to communicate the breach in security that had allowed McCarthy to overhear their conversation that evening.

Carlos began the conversation. "I thought you were only going to call me if there was an emergency. You were so fucking adamant about it."

"Well," Will responded hesitantly, "we've had a few problems come up that I thought you should be aware of."

"Go on," Carlos said bitingly.

"I'm just going to cut to the chase," Will hurriedly continued. "Jack McCarthy, one of my campaign staff members, happened to overhear our phone conversation the other night."

Before Will could continue, Carlos exploded on the other end of the line. "What the fuck do you mean he happened to overhear our phone conversation? I thought you were in your office on a secure line."

"I was. But my secretary forgot to hit the scrambler and then left her desk, which allowed McCarthy to pick up her receiver and listen in."

"Jesus Christ, Hawkins. This is a fucking mess that needs immediate attention."

"Calm down, Carlos. It's already been taken care of."

Carlos was silent on the other end of the line.

"In addition to McCarthy overhearing our plan, he also went to our Assistant Chief of Staff Steve Bess and shared what he heard."

The other end of the line was still silent, except for some heavy breathing.

"John Rollins came to the same conclusion you did; this situation needed immediate attention. So, as of this morning, both McCarthy and Bess have been silenced."

"I like the sound of that, Will, but I have to ask exactly what do you mean by silenced?"

"Steve Bess's official cause of death, without question, will be ruled a heart attack. He was given Dizanene in a sports drink sample at his health club. Dizanene is a—"

"I know what Dizanene is. It's a poison as lethal as strychnine, but it dissolves in the bloodstream in a matter of minutes, giving the impression that cardiac arrest was the cause of death."

Will involuntarily shuddered. It made him uncomfortable to think that Pendrill was so casually aware of an agent of death that he himself had only heard of a few days prior.

"What about McCarthy?" Carlos pressed.

"He's also out of our way, but his untimely death was anything but natural," Will quipped. "It would have been beyond coincidental to have two relatively young men on the campaign staff die of natural causes on the same day. So we created a more complex scenario to cover our tracks."

"I'm not looking for a suspense novel here, Will. How did he die?"

"We rigged his car to explode the next time he turns the key. In fact, it should have happened this morning."

"You what? How in the fuck do you plan on covering up an asinine move like that?"

"We have friends in the press," Will said in a calm voice. "We leaked a story to our contact yesterday, explaining that the campaign was investigating Jack McCarthy's involvement in a major drug smuggling operation. We're obviously supposed to be keeping it very hush-hush, but a small story ran in the metro section of this morning's paper. The minor damage this will do to the campaign will clearly validate our lack of involvement."

Carlos was calming down. Though he still wasn't happy about the method, he had to admit to himself he was more than a little impressed.

Will continued, "And this is the point where I was hoping to get a little help from you."

"Oh, really," Carlos responded sarcastically, "and what might that be?"

"Would it be fair to assume that you have a contact in the Dallas Police Department's narcotics division?"

"That would be a fair assumption."

"Would this person be at a level where he or she might be able to influence the department's interest in a certain case? Or better yet, backdate the initial investigation form?"

Again, Carlos was impressed with the planning that had preceded the actual car bombing.

"Our philosophy, Will," he answered, "is that the only person worth owning is one who can make things happen."

"Good," Will said. "If you can have your people verify the McCarthy narcotics investigation, then I think we can put these issues behind us."

"Done," Carlos answered, "but let me make one thing perfectly clear, Will. If you plan any more stunts like this without my knowledge, you and I are going to have a problem."

Will's initial reaction was, who in the fuck does he think he is? But before he could actually say anything, his political instincts reminded him who Carlos Pendrill was. He was not someone to be toyed with. Will could feel the hair on the back of his neck stand. The two men quickly agreed on next steps and hung up.

In Mexico City, Carlos leaned back confidently in his chair. Barring any further unforeseen events, the next president of the United States was now, most definitely, his.

o o o

Greg Larson and John Sterling had agreed to meet early Saturday morning at Barbec's near White Rock Lake. Larson had gone for a bike ride around the lake, and when he arrived at the popular breakfast eatery, he was shocked to see a long line of people in bike shorts already waiting for a table. He glanced at the line to see if Sterling had arrived yet. No luck. So he wandered to the back of the line, clearly feeling the fatigue in his legs after a fifteen-mile trek from his home and around the lake.

He found himself wishing he didn't have to ride home after breakfast. Once stationed at the rear of what appeared to be a ten- to fifteen-minute line, he heard a tapping of glass coming from behind him. He turned and, through the window, saw John Sterling already seated at a corner table in the restaurant. Larson made his way through the crowd of Saturday morning regulars and sat down across from the disheveled researcher he had come to respect immensely.

"How long have you been here?" Larson asked once he was seated.

"About thirty minutes," Sterling answered blandly. "Thought I would read the paper before you got here. It feels like I've been out of touch with the rest of the world lately."

"You've been out of touch with the rest of the world for twenty years," Larson joked.

"Eat shit," Sterling laughed. "You should be happy. I've been camped out in front of my computer screen just getting to know the Hawkins family."

"Glad you brought that up, John. Find anything interesting?"

"I've got to be honest. I've been striking out. In fact, until this morning, I didn't have anything new to report."

"Why, what happened this morning?"

Sterling handed the Metro Section of *The Dallas Free Press* to Larson. There on page two was the story about the Hawkins campaign's investigation into Jack McCarthy's alleged involvement with a large-scale drug smuggling operation. As Larson read the story, his smile appeared to get bigger by the minute.

"This is friggin' fantastic!" Greg exclaimed. "Drug smuggling at presidential campaign headquarters. That, coupled with the Pendrill connection, is the thread we pull that begins the unraveling of our illustrious senator. We've got to get more on this McCarthy. We might be able to use him to our advantage."

"I've got to tell you, Greg. I've been looking into the entire campaign staff for quite some time. They're all pretty clean."

"Well, obviously this McCarthy has some skeletons. His own employer is looking into his dealings. Keep digging on him. This is the kind of lead that will help us reach the promised land. A chink in the Hawkins armor! Let's deal that pompous fucking family a serious setback."

The two men agreed to reconvene the next day. The rest of breakfast was filled with friendly banter, both men understanding that the break they were looking for had just landed in their laps.

# twenty-six

Will Hawkins was feeling more confident than he had in days. The plan to eliminate the leak of his involvement with Carlos Pendrill was well under way. He had effectively managed the communication of the plan to Carlos, something he hadn't been looking forward to. Pendrill had agreed to enlist his high-level contact in the Dallas Police Department to help explain the McCarthy car bombing which, if things went according to plan, would happen sometime that morning. And he was now waiting for a call from David Ellis to finalize the details surrounding his alliance with The Future State Foundation. Life was good.

Just at that moment the phone rang. Stephanie was transferring David Ellis to Will's private line. Will felt a twinge of frustration at the sound of Stephanie's voice. He should have fired her ass for incompetence, but he and John Rollins had decided that if they never acknowledged the incident with Stephanie, the infamous phone call would never be identified beyond McCarthy and Bess. Will quickly shifted his attention back to the ringing phone. "Will Hawkins," he answered in a firm voice.

"Senator Hawkins, it's David Ellis."

The two men exchanged pleasantries before they got to the meat of the conversation. Will broke the ice. "David, I've thought a lot about our alliance. I think the timing is right to announce it to the press."

"I would have to disagree," David stated. "The key to this announcement is timing. If we don't make the announcement in conjunction with some significant environmental event, we run the risk of getting lost on page two or worse. And that wouldn't be good for either of us."

Will didn't immediately respond. Lost in his private thoughts surrounding the impending environmental disasters, his silence, while unintended, had the desired effect of making David Ellis nervous. Ellis was also quiet, trying to brainstorm a recovery strategy with Hawkins. He'd been playing the take-it-or-leave-it part for so long, he hadn't considered what he would do if Hawkins got frustrated and told him to pound sand. But at his very height of insecurity, Will broke the silence.

"I agree, David. Let's wait for a worthy event that will ensure maximum press coverage surrounding our announcement. But we can't afford to wait too long."

Confidence quickly restored, Ellis again went on the offensive. "I'm glad we can agree on the strategy. But I will tell you when the time is right. I've spent the last several years managing the press to my advantage, and I'm not willing to turn over the reins of the foundation's future to some press-secretary lackey you hired less than six months ago."

While his assessment of the Hawkins campaign's press credentials were accurate, Will was not about to let Ellis speak to him that way. "Mr. Ellis, I, too, have spent the past several years managing the press. I am more than willing to work with you on the timing of the announcement. But," Will's voice rose, "if you ever fucking talk to me like that again, not only will I immediately dissolve any association we may have, I will actively pursue any and all opportunities to bury you and the publicity-seeking machine you call The Future State Foundation."

Ellis was stunned and appropriately put in his place. He was also ready to respond, but, before he could utter the first line of his counterattack, John Rollins burst into Will Hawkins's office unannounced, without knocking and obviously distraught. He looked as if he'd seen a ghost. Will knew that whatever news he was delivering, it clearly took precedence over the banter that was taking place in his conversation with Ellis.

"David," Will stated quickly, "I've just received an emergency interruption that requires my immediate attention. I apologize, but I'll have to call Monday and reschedule the remainder of our discussion."

o o o

Before Ellis could respond, he heard the distinct click of disconnection. While it pissed him off to be dismissed so quickly, he was also relieved because the conversation with Hawkins had him on his heels. A delay in the conclusion of their discussion would clearly allow him to further strategize an amicable resolution.

o o o

"What's wrong?" Will asked Rollins, clearly frustrated by the interruption.

"We missed McCarthy and got his girlfriend."

Hawkins was stunned. The confidence he had gained during his morning conversations with Pendrill and Ellis escaped him like air leaving a punctured balloon. He was nearly hyperventilating.

"When did it happen?"

"Just now. We had a spotter down the street to verify the hit. There was nothing he could do but watch."

"Fuck!" Hawkins screamed. "We better figure out something quick, or we're dead!"

o o o

Jack McCarthy had his hands on his knees, watching the blood from his face drip off the end of his nose. His mind was racing to assimilate what he had just witnessed. The small piece of material lying next to his right toe looked familiar: a piece of his sweatshirt that Carrie had been wearing this morning.

The reality of the situation hit him like a gut punch from a heavy-weight boxer. He began to vomit, realizing that pieces of the woman he loved were strewn all over his front yard. He fumbled for the phone and dialed 911. After what seemed like forever, the dispatcher finally came on the line.

"My car exploded. My girlfriend . . . she's gone. Please hurry."

Jack hung up and began to sob. He staggered to the front porch and sat on the step. He tried to focus on what had just happened. Cars don't just explode.

Then, for the second time in less than five minutes, the retching that accompanied an overwhelming realization hit him. The car had obviously been rigged to explode! It had been meant for him.

The campaign knew he knew.

They had planned to kill him and got Carrie instead. The anger that instantly grew inside of him was unprecedented. Without hesitation, he knew at that moment Will Hawkins would pay for this. Every waking moment would be dedicated to avenging Carrie's senseless death.

Jack could hear the sirens. The police and the now-useless ambulance would be here in seconds. He was contemplating his next steps when it dawned on him that he had to reach Steve Bess. If they had gone after Jack, they would surely go after Steve as well. Or, had Steve Bess betrayed him? Yesterday, that didn't seem possible. But today, he wasn't sure who to trust.

As Jack continued to stare at the ground, he noticed two black boots directly in front of him. The first officer had arrived and was looking down at Jack impassively.

"Sir, are you with us? I mean, are you capable of responding to any questions?"

Jack nodded slightly. "I'm here, I just don't understand." Then he began to sob.

The next hour was a whirlwind of activity. Police, paramedics, and lab specialists were everywhere. The cuts on Jack's face were treated, and a number of police representatives asked him a multitude of questions, different questions that were intended to get at the same answers, questions that were designed to trip him up. Why did he feel like he was on trial here? He'd just lost a woman he loved dearly, and they were treating him like he was a criminal. It was all very frustrating, but he was too emotionally drained to fight back.

As his mind went in and out of focus, Jack noticed a very petite, attractive female walking toward him. The only reason he had noticed her was that she didn't seem to fit in. She headed straight toward him, very businesslike.

"Mr. McCarthy, I'm Kate Anson. I'm the homicide detective assigned to this case."

Jack was speechless. He'd never thought about a woman, much less a beautiful woman, being a homicide detective. She began again, with the same basic line of questioning. Obviously, she'd already been briefed on his previous answers, and she was looking for a way to get a different answer, to get some new information that had yet to be uncovered. The police tactic of trying to wear down a witness—a suspect!—was beginning to piss him off.

Jack looked up at the detective and said, "Look, Ms. Anson, I've been through a lot this morning, and I'm pretty fucking tired of answering the same questions over and over again."

"Well, Mr. McCarthy, I've just arrived at the scene, and I'm in charge of this investigation. So, I'll ask as many questions as I like as many times as I like, and you'll answer them."

They stared at each other with contempt.

"In fact," she continued, "the questions for you have just begun. This isn't your run-of-the-mill neighborhood incident. You're going to have to accompany me downtown."

"Am I under arrest?" Jack asked, surprised.

"Not yet, but that could change."

Jack stood up silently and followed her to an unmarked car.

## twenty-seven

Will Hawkins was still trying to grasp the unbelievable fact that he had caused the death of
an innocent bystander. He felt as if he were
losing control of the situation. John Rollins
was pacing back and forth across the office,
waiting for Will to regain his composure. After several moments, Will
began to speak. "We've got to get our hands on McCarthy. It won't be
long before he figures out that the bomb was intended for him."

"I agree," Rollins added, "but how do we pry him away from the
police without calling attention to ourselves and before he tells them
what he knows?"

Both men sat in silence, looking for an answer.

"I think I have something," Rollins finally blurted out. "But we've
got to move fast."

"I'm open to anything. What are you thinking?"

"Well, Pendrill has a police contact in the narcotics division, right?"

"Right."

"What if we get in touch with this contact via Pendrill and have
McCarthy detained within police headquarters based on his alleged
involvement with a very powerful, Dallas-based narcotics ring? Then
before they have a chance to question him, two of our guys, posing as

DEA agents, pick him up for a transfer to their own holding facility. Then we have him."

"What do we do once we have him?"

"We make him disappear. Then we plant a story in *The Dallas Free Press* regarding McCarthy's abduction by some of his high-powered drug friends and, well, just another casualty of the Dallas drug wars."

"That's going to be highly embarrassing to the Dallas Police Department and complicated for Carlos."

"Yeah, that crossed my mind," Rollins continued, "but the stakes are that high. Pendrill will be pissed. But he'll conclude that potentially compromising his contact in narcotics is ever so much more appealing than McCarthy telling the world the conversation he overheard."

"Then what?" Will asked, too numb to contribute to the plan.

"We issue a statement from you," Rollins said in a frustrated tone. "We acknowledge to the world that the campaign made a bad choice. We briefly discuss our screening process prior to entering into any employment agreements but that the process had obviously let this one slip through the cracks. But the clincher will be how shocked and disappointed you are that you could be so naïve. That you befriended a talented young man and were betrayed by him. That this incident has solidified your resolve to fight drugs in a manner not seen from a president in the last thirty years: your increased commitment to making a difference on the war against drugs."

Rollins was staring at Hawkins, silently urging him to pull it together, to understand that it wasn't over but that they had to move quickly.

"Do you think it can work?" Will asked in a monotone voice.

"Do you have any better ideas?"

o o o

Jack McCarthy and Kate Anson were just pulling on to Central Expressway, heading south toward downtown. They had yet to say a word to each other since getting into the car.

Kate spoke first. "So, Mr. McCarthy, do you have any idea why someone would rig your car with explosives? It's not exactly a run-of-the-mill response to a simple neighborhood dispute."

"You can call me Jack."

"All right, Jack. Do you know why someone would want you dead?"

The tone of her voice indicated that she believed he knew something. This was not the type of incident where you could play dumb and people would believe you. Jack sat in the passenger seat, silently trying to focus on what he should do next. His options were limited. The police were treating him like a suspect. He had nowhere to turn. At that instant, Jack decided to roll the dice and confide in the beautiful homicide detective sitting to his left.

"As a matter of fact, Ms. Anson, I have a real good idea who would want to eliminate me."

Jack spent the next five minutes summarizing his involvement in the campaign—the innocent way in which he overheard the candidate's outrageous plan and how he had confided in Steve Bess. Saying Bess's name sent a sudden chill through him like an electric current.

He blurted out, "We need to call Steve Bess! He was the only other person who knew the story. He is in serious danger."

"Or," Kate responded, "he could be on the other side."

Jack nodded, knowing he'd already thought the same thing. "But if he's not involved and I don't warn him . . ."

Kate handed Jack her cell phone without either of them saying another word. Jack dialed Bess's home number. It rang endlessly. Jack was about to hang up, wondering why the answering machine hadn't picked up, when a faint woman's voice said, "Hello."

"Jenny?" Jack said questioningly. She didn't sound like herself.

"Yes, who's this?"

"Jenny, it's Jack McCarthy. Is Steve home?"

Jenny Bess began to sob.

"Jenny, what's wrong? What's going on there?"

As he was asking these questions, Jack and Kate were staring at each other, knowing something terrible was about to be communicated.

"Steve's dead, Jack. He had a heart attack at the club this morning. He was gone before the paramedics arrived."

Jack tried to remain calm. "Oh my God, Jen, what can I do to help?" He was trying to act natural in this surreal situation.

"Nothing right now, Jack. My parents just arrived."

"Jesus, Jen, I don't know what to say other than my thoughts and prayers are with you and the kids. I'll call this afternoon to see if there's anything I can do."

Without waiting for her reply, Jack hit the end button on the cell phone, staring at Kate in disbelief. She knew what he was thinking as she turned away from the police station.

Detective Anson parked her department-issued Chevy Impala on the south side of Adair's, a dive bar and burger joint that predated its hip, Deep Ellum surroundings by nearly thirty years. Jack looked over at the detective questioningly.

"I think we should talk further before we go to the station," Kate said.

They entered the dingy restaurant from Main Street. It was still relatively early this sunny Saturday morning, but a handful of Adair's regulars were already drinking beer and playing pool. They grabbed a corner booth and stared at each other, wondering who would start.

Finally Kate broke the silence. "You know, in all my years as a homicide detective, your story is the most outrageous that I have ever heard. But, for some strange reason, I believe you."

"Well, it's way too wild to make up," Jack said, smiling a little. "I can't believe this is happening. Just a few months ago, I was a regular guy going to work every day, reading about things that happen to other people. Now, this morning, Carrie was murdered by a car bomb meant for me." Jack bowed his head and began to cry.

After a few minutes Kate touched his arm and said, "I'm very sorry about your girlfriend, Jack. I know it's not possible to understand how you're feeling right now, so I won't even tell you I'm trying. But I do know that if your story is accurate, and I believe it is, we've got to do something . . . quickly."

"Got any ideas?" Jack asked, trying to regain his composure.

"Yes, here's what we're going to do. You and I go to the station. I take your statement as the lead investigator on the case. You profess to have no idea why anyone would want to hurt you. With no evidence to link you to a crime, we'll have to let you go. That will give me time to reach Frank Lahey who's the assistant chief of police. He's also a friend of my father's; in fact, he's like a second father to me. He's hunting this weekend, but he'll be back late Sunday night."

Jack watched in amazement as Kate Anson rattled off the plan while barely taking a breath.

"Then, once I hook you up with Uncle Frank, you two can figure out what to do about that sonofabitch Will Hawkins."

"What about you?" Jack asked.

"I think you'll need a little more firepower than just another female detective in the homicide department . . . if you know what I mean," she said, smiling.

"Why are you doing this?" Jack asked again, not knowing what to think of her or the situation.

"Well, let's just say I had a bad experience with our illustrious Senator Hawkins that helps me believe your story."

"What happened?" he asked.

"It's not important," she responded. "Let's just make sure we nail him."

# twenty-eight

Ian McKay was strolling down the concourse at Austin-Bergstrom International Airport. The airport was new and clean and had a certain charm about it. As he passed the sculpture claiming Austin as the world's greatest music city, it made him wish he were here for sightseeing, not old and unpleasant family business. McKay had come to the Texas capital with a plan to ensure he was right up front at the conclusion of Senator Will Hawkins's upcoming Austin campaign speech, as listed on his campaign website. He needed to be in a position to pass the good senator a note. The note would be simple and to the point:

> *You killed my brother in London many years ago.*
> *I know who you are.*
> *I want $25 million.*
> *Contact the McSorley room at the Austin Four Seasons.*

As McKay exited the airport, he hailed a cab so he could head downtown. He was staying at the Driskill Hotel on Sixth Street. In addition to its millions of dollars in recent renovations, the Driskill was famous for its party location and for a certain governor's wife's legendary entrance to a long-past New Year's Eve Ball. It seems the governor's wife had started drinking a little early and tripped at the top of the grand staircase in the lobby, tumbling to the bottom as helpless onlookers waited to see if she was injured or dead. She rose to her feet, straightened her gown, raised her arms above her head, and yelled, "Ta da!" The crowd cheered, and no one even noticed the governor slowly descend the staircase, shaking his head.

Ian McKay arrived at the Driskill around noon. As luck would have it, a room was available for early check-in, and he immediately changed into running clothes so that he could inconspicuously scope the next day's speech location. Ian walked out of the hotel's front door, looked left, and began running down Sixth Street, nearly abandoned at this time of day. When he reached Congress, he turned right and was heading straight toward the state capitol. As he closed in on the steps of the capitol, Ian slowed to a walk, taking in the surroundings. The setup for the campaign rally had already begun. He used his reconnaissance experience to anticipate the security plans. It was already clear in his mind where they would place the stage, where the crowd would be located, and, most importantly, where the candidate would greet his well-wishers.

The plan was now complete in McKay's mind. He would rise early and stay close to the assembly area until the crowd began to form. Once enough people had arrived, he would find a spot right against the temporary fence and wait patiently until the unwitting candidate walked right up to him and shook his hand.

o o o

Jack McCarthy and Kate Anson had finished their restaurant conversation and decided it was time to make their appearance at Dallas Police Headquarters. As they entered the station through the main door on Commerce Street, they were intercepted by a large, middle-aged man in a suit that looked like he'd been wearing it for the past year and a half. The man was Brian Hatcher, the head of DPD's Narcotics division for more than ten years. "We'll take it from here, Kate."

Kate Anson was stunned. "What are you talking about, Brian? This is my case, and I'm not even sure why Narcotics would be involved."

"Well, I guess you didn't have time to read the paper this morning. Mr. McCarthy here is suspected of and now under investigation for his involvement in a major drug trafficking ring."

Kate shot a nasty look at Jack, whose mouth hung open with shock and amazement.

Kate quickly recovered. "Brian, regardless of the motive, this is still a murder investigation. The last time I checked, that would be Homicide's jurisdiction."

"Well, normally I would agree, Kate. But the high-profile nature of the suspect, coupled with his employer's very public stance against drugs, has backed the chief into a corner. He wants to find this trafficking ring and dismantle it. Quickly."

Kate Anson was pissed. Jack McCarthy had used her. He had played her like a fiddle, and that was emotionally devastating because she had opened up to him, which was a very rare occurrence in her personal or professional life. To top it off, the egomaniacs from Narcotics were stealing her case, and it was obvious there was very little she could do about it. So, as both men stared at her, waiting for the inevitable explosion of anger, she instantly decided she would not humor them with the expected response. As she eyed each of the men coldly, she turned on her heel and began to walk away.

As she looked over her shoulder, she shot back a sarcastic, "Good luck."

Neither of the men was sure whom it was directed toward.

When Kate had disappeared around the corner, Brian Hatcher turned to Jack and issued him the Miranda rights. When he was done, he silently, gently turned Jack around and handcuffed him.

As Hatcher led Jack to the first-floor interrogation room, Jack turned and asked, "What the fuck is going on here? I have no knowledge of any drug smuggling operation, and you know it."

"I'm just following orders, Mr. McCarthy. I'm sure if you are innocent, the justice system will issue the appropriate verdict. But until then, I suggest you get yourself a good lawyer." With that, Hatcher shoved Jack into a barren room with two chairs, a table, and a government-issue two-way mirror. As the door closed behind him, Jack was left with his thoughts of loneliness and helplessness. He thought about Carrie and began to sob.

Brian Hatcher entered his office and closed the door. He dialed the numbers provided to him earlier that morning. When he heard the familiar tone indicating it was time to speak, his message was brief and to the point.

"It's done. He's in interrogation room 1B."

Hatcher smiled to himself. That was the easiest $100,000 he'd ever made.

# twenty-nine

reg Larson and Tom Johnson were scheduled to meet on Saturday afternoon to discuss Larson's progress on the Will Hawkins series. What they hadn't expected was the incident earlier that morning that had completely reshaped the approach to the high-profile assignment given to Larson.

"This is absolutely unbelievable!" Larson exclaimed, almost out of breath. "This morning I'm meeting John Sterling for breakfast to discuss his research progress." Larson paused to gather his thoughts. "Sterling's awesome, by the way. Anyway, he shares with me the small article in the Metro section of the *Free Press* regarding McCarthy's alleged drug ties, and by the time we finish breakfast, McCarthy's car has exploded with his girlfriend in it. Looks like Jack has some really nasty friends."

Johnson nodded. "Yeah, it looks like he's in pretty deep. But he sure doesn't appear to be your typical drug trafficker."

"I agree, Tom. That's why I'm adamantly opposed to using my byline to report on this situation."

"You've got to be kidding me! A top aide to the front-running Democratic candidate is involved in drug trafficking, his girlfriend blows up in his car in a trendy Dallas neighborhood, and you're going to take a pass? I can't believe what I'm hearing!"

"I know I'm leaving you hanging here, Tom, but if I do this story, I can't reel in the big one. I want an exclusive with Will Hawkins, and if I have any involvement in negatively impacting the campaign via this McCarthy story, he'll deny me."

Johnson contemplated Larson's reasoning. "He might deny you anyway. Then you have nothing."

At that moment, Larson considered sharing the Will Hawkins/Carlos Pendrill connection with Johnson but quickly decided against it. "I think I can get him, Tom. In fact, I'm staking my career on it."

"What do you have that you're not telling me about?"

Greg smiled. "Nothing yet, Tom. But with the help of Chambers's buddy Sterling, I'm hoping that's going to change very quickly."

The discussion surrounding Jack McCarthy's involvement in drug trafficking and the death of his girlfriend lasted another ten minutes. Tom Johnson knew that he was not going to persuade Larson to do the story. Finally, he relented and agreed to assign the piece to someone else.

Larson smiled. "Thanks, Tom; you're not going to regret this. When I finish this one, Chambers will have the Pulitzer Prize he's been coveting since my last one."

Both men laughed.

"Well, I hope you're right, Greg. It'll be both our asses if this plan backfires. So do me a favor; bring home the big one, and make us both look smart."

"Deal," Larson quickly conceded, lost in his own thoughts.

Will Hawkins and Carlos Pendrill, roommates and friends in graduate school. Larson knew that would make some news. And now this McCarthy thing. What a tangled web Hawkins had woven.

Tom Johnson watched Larson as he stared off into space. He couldn't help but wonder what was going on in the reporter's odd, brilliant mind.

o o o

Jack McCarthy watched his interrogator and couldn't help but view him as a movie character. The detective was balding and twenty pounds overweight, with a well-worn dress shirt and his tie loosened to give his thick neck some extra room. The detective was doing his best "good cop" imitation, including taking Jack's handcuffs off.

The one thing that wasn't dreamlike during his incessant questioning was the primal fear Jack felt as the detective made statements like, "You mean to tell me you are in no way associated with the Torres drug ring? I read the papers, Jack. I also know that it's extremely rare for innocent citizens to have their cars rigged with explosives. Give me a break, man. I want to help you find the guys who blew up your car."

Jack was about to respond by telling the detective to get him a lawyer when the interrogation room door burst open.

Two men in dark suits, white shirts, and black ties entered the room. They were big, impeccably dressed, and very official-looking.

As they closed the door behind them, the Dallas Police Department detective exclaimed, "Who the hell are you?"

"FBI," answered the first man. "We've been ordered to pick up Mr. McCarthy. This is now a federal case."

"Like hell it is!" answered the detective. "No one told me to release this suspect to anyone."

"Listen, sir, we're just following orders."

The man continued to speak as he approached the detective.

"Now we can do this the easy way, or," and as smoothly as if he were still carrying on a casual conversation, the man delivered one open-handed blow to the detective's neck, dropping him like a limp rag doll.

Jack was stunned. But before he could recover, the second man expertly put a small, well-concealed pistol in his back and said, "All right, McCarthy, it's time for you to come with us."

Jack felt numb. He had no idea how to react. But as the two men marched him out of the interrogation room toward the front entrance, he began to yell. "Something is wrong here, people! These men are taking me against my will. They are not FBI. They must be working for Will Hawkins."

Jack was perplexed. No one seemed to pay any attention to his ranting and raving. Then it dawned on him that he had played it exactly the way they had hoped—just another criminal exclaiming his innocence. No one in the station noticed because it happened every day. In fact, his reaction to the men escorting him out of the building ended up being the perfect cover.

Once outside, the two men grabbed Jack and manhandled him toward a nondescript black sedan. Jack had no idea what to do. However, he was convinced that if they got him in the car, there was a good chance he was done. So, without thinking through it any further, Jack struck like a cornered animal. His first black-belt move was to disarm the man with the gun in his back. Jack quickly stepped to the side, grabbing the gunman by the wrist. Using the man's own mass against him, he swung him toward the street, dislocating his shoulder as if he were a mannequin. The man dropped the gun into the gutter and fell to the ground in excruciating pain.

This move, however, had given the other aggressor time to react. He lunged at Jack, grabbing his throat with all his strength. The imposter agent was big and extremely strong but only marginally skilled at the martial arts. While in a significant amount of pain, Jack patiently waited for the appropriate moment and again used the man's own weight against him. Jack dropped to one knee and rolled the man to his right. In one expert move that surprised even Jack, the man was on his back. Jack gave him two short jabs to the jaw, knocking him unconscious.

Jack got to his feet quickly and scanned the area for more trouble. Surprisingly, the street was relatively quiet, and no one seemed to notice the brief scuffle. The gunman with the dislocated shoulder was beginning to regain his composure, so Jack took off in a sprint. Fifteen yards later, as he rounded the corner onto Harwood Street, Jack slowed to a brisk walk to avoid undue attention.

Just when he thought he was in the clear, a female voice from behind said, "Stop right where you are; you're under arrest."

Jack was about to explain when a car squealed quickly around the corner, causing Kate Anson to turn, startled by the commotion. At nearly the same moment, Jack acted out of sheer instinct, tackling Kate to the ground just as an automatic weapon opened fire, spraying the building wall behind them with dozens of bullets. As the car continued to hurtle down the street, Kate jumped to her feet, confused by the activity of the past few seconds. Then she quickly regained her composure and realized that an attempt had just been made on both their lives. Without a spoken word, the two looked into each other's eyes and dashed for her car at the corner.

# thirty

Will Hawkins and John Rollins were together in Hawkins's downtown office. Will sat facing the telephone while Rollins paced back and forth. The voice coming through the telephone speaker box was Detective Brian Hatcher. As the conversation progressed, the agitation and intensity in the room grew exponentially. Finally, the information being delivered became too much for Rollins. He sprang toward the phone like a lion pouncing on its prey. His face was no more than twelve inches from the speakerphone.

"Do you mean to tell me that not only are you so incompetent that your two highly trained men let McCarthy escape, but then your solution was to gun him down on the street while he's in the presence of another police officer? You must be the stupidest fucking detective to ever get a badge. What were you thinking?"

"McCarthy told her everything," Hatcher responded. "She came to see me right after I made the call. She told me how stupid she felt believing his far-fetched story, but she couldn't shake the feeling that he was telling the truth. The plan was to get her later and just have her disappear, but circumstances out of my control put them at the same place at the same time, so we went for it."

"And missed," Rollins added sarcastically. "I'll call you back."

With that, Rollins punched the button on the speakerphone, ending the call abruptly.

Will Hawkins sat quietly. He had not participated in the conversation because they did not want Hatcher to know he was there. The look on his face told the whole story. He was angry, scared, and frustrated all at the same time.

Rollins looked at Will and said, "I'll handle this. You get down to Austin and rehearse your speech. Tomorrow's rally is your most important yet. Don't let this be a distraction."

"No, no, John, not at all." Will spoke with venom in his voice. "Just another campaign detail. Listen, John, you better handle this, or the next big speech I give will be following my sentencing. So please do me a favor; don't fuck it up. And, oh, by the way, don't tell my father."

o o o

Kate Anson and Jack McCarthy were driving down Ross Avenue in downtown Dallas, wondering what to do next. Kate was completely unprepared to acknowledge that an attempt had just been made on her life right outside the station. Jack understood her reluctance, but it was imperative that he get through to her and recruit her to his side.

"Kate, I know it's difficult to comprehend, but I've had a little more time to deal with the situation. Will Hawkins is involved with some very bad people who are determined to stop me. Or, I should now say, us."

"Jack, I'm beginning to understand just how deep we're in, but I'm at a loss for what to do next."

The two sat silent for a few moments, lost in their own thoughts. Finally, Kate suggested she contact Frank Lahey, the old friend of her father's she had mentioned earlier.

"No," Jack blurted out, stopping her in mid-sentence. "At this point, I don't trust anyone." Jack paused, noticing that Kate looked hurt by his last comment. "That is, except for you."

Kate shrugged, "Got any bright ideas?"

"The key is to find someone who would personally or professionally benefit from Hawkins's exposure. Has he had an affair or mistreated someone who has a personal vendetta?" He eyed Kate, waiting for a response.

She knew he was watching her reaction, so she finally turned to him and said, "Okay, yes, I had a humiliating experience with Senator Will Hawkins many years ago. He made an aggressive, drunken pass at me, which I resisted vehemently. He called me a 'teasin' bitch' and walked away. So admittedly, I've hated him ever since, but that doesn't give me the credibility necessary to make these types of accusations."

"True," Jack responded thoughtfully. "Regardless of your detective status, Hawkins's insiders would discredit you as quickly as they did me."

"What about the media or the Republicans, both would obviously kill to possess this type of information?"

Jack was quiet for a moment and then responded, "That's it. We contact the president."

"We what?" Kate exclaimed. "Are you out of your mind?"

"Think about it," Jack said. "What better way to ensure that the story is not lost or suppressed? President Hughes would directly benefit from the release of the story, not to mention that he has the power to make sure the public is informed."

"How would we get to him?"

"I'm thinking. First, we need to get in close proximity. Same town, same airport, something. Next, we get a message to him or his chief of staff explaining that an adviser to Will Hawkins wants to see him regarding something of utmost importance."

Kate interrupted. "But everyone thinks you're a drug dealer. Imagine what type of spin is already being created at the station."

"You're right. But if I explain that what I know is why I was framed, they'll have to at least listen. And once we get them to listen, they're going to be interested."

"What if they won't see us?" Kate asked skeptically.

"They'll have to. Anyway, what are our options?"

"All right, then," Kate said, feigning energy. "Let's find the president."

"Now, we need a copy of the presidential campaign schedule," Jack said.

"How about the Internet?" Kate responded sarcastically.

Jack laughed and added, "I guess that's the easy part. The hard part is finding somewhere to stay tonight where they won't find us."

After minutes of silence as each of them racked their brains for a safe spot, Jack spoke first. "Carrie's parents have a lake house out at Cedar Creek. It's secluded, and I know where they keep the key. They're not returning until tomorrow morning, so I'll just leave a message on their machine, and we'll be out of there before they even get it."

"Why leave a message?"

"Exactly! I want them to think the same thing—how odd it is that I left a message, how that type of action is not consistent with a man on the run."

Kate raised her eyebrows, ready to further question his logic, but decided to let it drop. They began the drive east on I-30 in silence, both of them contemplating what the future had in store.

# thirty-one

Ian McKay awoke at 5:00 a.m. in his room at the Driskill Hotel. He methodically got his belongings together in an effort to make a quick exit if necessary. Will Hawkins's speech on the steps of the capitol wasn't until noon, but McKay had already decided that if he wanted to ensure his place in the receiving line, he needed to be there by 7:00 a.m.

When Ian stepped out onto Sixth Street, it was already hot and humid. He began the ten-block stroll up Congress to the capitol. With each block, his emotional intensity built. Ian was finally going to look into the eyes of the man who had beat his brother to death more than two decades ago.

Ian approached the spot where he envisioned the meeting would take place. As he stood there, imagining what it would be like to stare into the eyes of an unknowing Will Hawkins, he reviewed the plan in his head: making sure he was right up against the restraining fence; catching the candidate's attention with a small sign proclaiming "The Hawkins Administration will change the world." Ian was sure the sign would catch the attention of the egomaniacal Hawkins, but it was also his attempt at a cruel joke. He knew in his heart that if elected, Senator Hawkins would find a way to fuck up his administration.

Once the senator approached, Ian would offer his hand, palming the incriminating note. The note would identify him as the brother of the man Hawkins killed in London a quarter-century earlier. It would demand a $25 million payment to his niece, the young woman who never knew her father because of him. It would instruct Hawkins to get a suite at the Four Seasons on Town Lake and wait for a call. Once contacted, Hawkins would be told to come to Lee Park in Dallas on Tuesday with a duffel bag full of unmarked, low-denomination bills. The final instructions were to come alone. If anything happened to disrupt the transaction, the press would be immediately notified of the unknown incident.

It would work. The $25 million would hurt them but wasn't debilitating to the Hawkins family. Young Will not becoming president—that would be completely unacceptable.

○ ○ ○

Jack McCarthy was in that barely conscious state of awareness just before a person fully awakes to his morning surroundings. It was 6:00 a.m. on Sunday. Jack and Kate had slept fewer than five hours, and it was a restless sleep at best. As Jack became aware of his surroundings, he realized that he was in his dead girlfriend's parents' lake house with a beautiful homicide detective resting on his shoulder. The surreal nature of his reality came rushing back to him. Jack tried to slide out from underneath Kate Anson without waking her but was unsuccessful.

Jack stood in the well-decorated but rustic great room of the lake house. Kate, having quickly gained her senses, asked, "What's going on? Where are you going?"

"Out to get a newspaper," Jack replied. "I was hoping to let you sleep until I got back."

Relieved that there wasn't something more sinister to his careful movement, Kate said she'd take a quick shower and see him when he returned.

As Jack drove the mile and a half down the bumpy dirt road that provided access to the lake house from State Highway 175, he couldn't shake the overwhelming feeling of inadequacy regarding what to do next. There was no one for him and Kate to trust and no definitive path for them to follow. Jack wheeled the unmarked police cruiser into the empty parking lot of the local Loaf and Jug.

When he entered, the man behind the counter gave him a loud, genuine "howdy" to which Jack replied, "How ya doing?"

He quickly realized that not only did he need a newspaper, but food was definitely in order as well. He quickly perused the fresh food counter and determined that in this case, the word fresh was used quite liberally. Following that line of thinking, he passed on the biscuits and gravy and grabbed a couple of bagels instead. Two bottles of orange juice, two coffees, and a *Dallas Free Press* followed next. As he stacked the various items on the counter, what he saw next nearly stopped his heart. The Sunday morning headline was, "Drug Shootout at Police HQ." Below the bold-type headline were two photographs: headshots of Kate and him. Jack quickly recovered from his initial shock, turned the paper over to conceal the photos from the man behind the counter, paid quickly, and headed toward the door.

Just as he reached for the door handle, the man behind the counter spoke. "Excuse me, sir. I take pride in knowing my customers. Haven't I seen you in here before?"

The answer was no, but he'd probably glanced at the morning paper and seen his photo on the front page. But Jack, having spent the past twenty years having to think on his feet, answered, "Yes. My girlfriend's folks have a place down on the lake, and we come out several times a year." Before the man could respond, Jack opened the door and left.

Jack's mind was reeling on the drive back to the lake. They needed to leave at once. He'd already left a message for Carrie's parents telling them he was going to stay there Saturday night. As soon as they saw the newspaper, they were sure to call the police. He also needed to ditch Kate's car. Every trooper in Texas was probably looking for the unmarked cruiser involved in yesterday's downtown Dallas shootout. Jack skidded to a stop on the gravel driveway, jumped out of the car, and ran inside to grab Kate. What he saw next stopped him in his tracks. In the corner of the room, tied to a kitchen chair, was Kate. Next to her was a large man in a dark suit casually pointing a gun at her head. The smile on his face indicated he was enjoying the moment.

"Welcome to the party, Mr. McCarthy. Kate and I were just talking about you."

"Who the fuck are you?" Jack barked in the most intimidating voice he could muster.

"I think you know the answer to that question, Mr. McCarthy. Please sit down."

Jack scanned the room as he moved toward the chair set up next to Kate. He quickly noticed a man out behind the house leaning against a black sedan. The man was obviously the lookout but seemed relatively uninterested and was assuming things were in control. Jack continued across the room as the man with the gun laughed at Jack's naïveté.

"You're probably wondering how we found you. You should never leave messages for friends or family when you're on the lam."

The comment felt like a blow to the stomach. His strategy to establish naïve innocence with Carrie's parents had backfired and put him and Kate in grave danger. The anger that accompanied this realization went off in him like an explosion. In one move, Jack covered the last three feet between himself and the gunman, grabbed the gun in a twisting motion, broke the man's arm, and dislocated his shoulder simultaneously. Then, with one blow to the back of the neck, the gunman crumpled to the floor.

Her eyes wide in amazement, Kate asked, "How did you do that?"

Jack responded, slightly out of breath, "Tae Kwan Do. I do it to stay in shape. I never thought I'd actually have to use it."

Kate smiled as Jack untied her. "Well, I'm glad you're vain enough to stay in shape." The two restrained the unconscious gunman while discussing a plan to escape their current situation.

The plan was fairly simple. They needed to get the attention of the man standing guard outside so that Jack could come in from behind and subdue him. The plan had one catch; Kate was the bait. As they were still discussing the pros and cons of Kate keeping the guard's attention, she was scanning the well-appointed lake house for an idea. When she began rummaging through the drawers of the second bedroom, she found what she was looking for. Less than a minute later, she exited from the bedroom wearing a very revealing one-piece swimsuit. Jack stopped in his tracks. She was stunning, but his reaction was not what Kate had expected.

"Take that thing off immediately. What do you think you're doing?"

Kate was taken aback. This was not the reaction she had expected, but before she responded, she realized the impetus for Jack's reaction: the swimsuit. It had obviously been Carrie's, and Jack was having a reaction to the guilt and pain that he had not yet been able to deal with.

Kate chose her words carefully. "The plan is simple, Jack. I sneak out the back door, slip into the water, swim to the neighbor's dock, and then saunter toward the man outside, keeping his interest directed toward me. You come in from behind and do your thing."

"I don't like it," Jack replied. "It's too dangerous for you to approach an armed man who's obviously here to harm us. Not to mention, that's a lot of open water between docks."

Kate smiled. She hadn't taken that into consideration, but she was clearly ready to give it a try. "Do you have any better ideas?" she said, looking at him, trying to understand his feelings.

He was momentarily silent but finally answered, "No."

Kate added a swim cap to her outfit to minimize the chances of the man outside recognizing her before Jack had a chance to approach from behind. She quietly exited the back door and slipped down the heavily wooded path to the dock. As she eased herself into the water, she realized it was farther than it looked from shore. The neighbor's dock was only a couple of hundred yards away across the lake, but now it appeared to be miles. Kate began to question whether she could make it. "No turning back now," she whispered to herself.

She began a quiet breaststroke toward her destination, always keeping an eye toward the guard leaning against his car. He appeared to be getting fidgety. Boredom, coupled with the edginess associated with waiting for his partner to exit the lake house, was taking its toll.

She was nearly there. Just a few more yards to go. She could just see the front hood of the Lincoln Town Car that had come for them, but the guard was not in sight. Her heart skipped a beat, thinking he had gotten restless and gone in to see what was taking so long. Before she had time to react, he reappeared.

"No time like the present," she said quietly and climbed the ladder on to the dock.

She could see the guard tense up as he spotted her immediately. Kate didn't want to raise his suspicion, so she didn't immediately acknowledge his presence. She wished she had a towel; the slight breeze in the air, working in conjunction with her adrenaline, had her trembling. What now? she thought. She needed to get his full attention for the next couple of minutes to allow Jack time to approach from behind. Then it came to her. She began a stretching routine on the dock that was half calisthenics, half gentlemen's club that she knew in her heart of hearts would keep any man's attention at least for a while.

After what seemed to Kate like an eternity, she ended her show and casually glanced toward the guard. At the appropriate moment, her body dramatically jerked in acknowledgement of the presence of someone else. She casually waved toward the guard and began a slow, seductive walk in his direction. He didn't move, mesmerized by the fact that his first human encounter since he arrived was an attractive woman in a swimsuit.

As she continued her slow, deliberate approach, Jack began his own approach from behind. Just as Kate was about to speak to the guard, not knowing what else to do, Jack pounced. His first shot to the neck, the one that had incapacitated the guard's partner not twenty minutes earlier, did not have the same effect. The man in the suit swung around in fury, ready to take on whatever had just hit him.

Jack squared up in his start position, awaiting the guard's first move. What he didn't expect was a physical response that communicated his opponent was also skilled at the martial arts. What took place over the next forty seconds looked like a fight straight out of a Bruce Lee movie. Hands and feet were flying more quickly than the eye could follow.

Most blows were blocked, with an occasional hand or foot connecting with its target.

Kate watched in fear, unable to move a muscle to help Jack in this brutal battle. All at once, the action stopped as Jack fell to his knees, obviously the victim of an intense blow to the midsection or somewhere nearby. As the man in the suit smiled and slowly approached Jack for the final blow, Jack suddenly sent a two-fisted uppercut to his groin. He doubled over, and Jack directed a savage, two-fisted blow to his jaw. He crumpled to the ground in a heap of black suit.

Jack and Kate exchanged glances and, without speaking a word, began to move the guard's massive body toward the lake house. Once inside, the two quickly tied his hands and feet in a manner similar to his partner. Once complete, the two checked their first conquest and were pleasantly surprised that the knots had actually tightened as planned when the guard struggled to get free.

As the two exited the front door, Jack turned to the one conscious guard, grinned, and said, "There's food in the fridge if you get hungry." He closed the door as Kate was already reaching toward the passenger door of her unmarked car. "Wait," Jack said, "they may have rigged the car. Besides, every Texas Ranger from here to Oklahoma will be looking for the fugitives in the unmarked police car."

The two fugitives scurried to the black Lincoln Town Car and drove down the dirt road toward their destiny. Less than twenty seconds into their trip, Kate let out a scream.

Jack slammed on the brakes, yelling, "What's the matter?"

Kate turned the front page of the *Free Press* toward Jack. He had forgotten, with the rest of the morning's events, that she had not yet seen her mug on the front page of the Sunday paper.

He responded, "Nice shots, huh?" and continued to drive.

"I can't believe this is fucking happening," Kate groaned.

They discussed their plan as they drove. President Hughes had a trip planned to Vail, Colorado, for a little vacation. His mentor from his first term in Congress, Gerald Ford, had originally introduced him to the splendors of the Vail Valley many years ago. During his time as president, Vail had become to him what Key West had been to Truman and what Cape Cod had been to Kennedy.

Jack and Kate's plan was to get to Colorado and somehow find a way to meet with him. But, first things first. They had to find another car, switch plates to be safe, and get some cash. They were hoping to find someone to cash a check; that would take longer to trace than a credit card. Once that was done, they would drive the twelve-plus hours to Colorado and meet the president of the United States. They both started to laugh hysterically . . . like that was going to be an easy meeting to get set up.

# thirty-two

Greg Larson walked to the end of the driveway of his modest Lakewood home. It was rare for him, but he had slept until almost 9:45 on a glorious Sunday morning. As he settled in to perform his weekly ritual of reading the Sunday *Free Press* cover to cover, the front page caught his attention. The photos of Jack McCarthy and Kate Anson immediately piqued his interest. This was the same Jack McCarthy who just yesterday was relegated to page two of the Metro section. Now he was front-page news and on the run with a Dallas Police Department homicide detective. It was getting more and more intriguing.

Larson devoured the story of the Will Hawkins aide, allegedly involved in a major drug trafficking organization. The violent way McCarthy's girlfriend had died, coupled with the midday shooting in downtown Dallas, sickened Larson. But at the same time, the adrenaline rush associated with the fact that he was on to something big left him almost giddy. He now had the ammunition he was desperately searching for. One fact was front-page news. The other, the fact that Carlos Pendrill was Will Hawkins's roommate, so far had not surfaced. He could not believe his luck. But much of the luck could actually be attributed to John Sterling, the '60s-throwback researcher who was the best he had ever worked with.

Larson knew in his heart the time had come. It was time to contact John Rollins and request a one-on-one interview with Will Hawkins. He would obviously have to deceive Rollins, telling him that as hard as he'd tried, no good dirt was uncovered on the fine senator. Assuming the Democrats agreed (and he knew they would), he would proceed with what appeared to be a standard interview. Then, without any hint of aggression, he would hit Will Hawkins with both barrels. He was imagining the conversation.

"Senator, is it true that the fugitive Jack McCarthy was a key part of your staff?"

He could hear the answer as if he were clairvoyant.

"Yes, Greg, he was. And no one was more shocked than I at Jack's alleged extracurricular activities."

"Well, Senator, is it also true that the world's most ruthless drug kingpin was your roommate and confidant in graduate school?"

Larson could picture the look on Hawkins's face. It would be priceless in more ways than one. But for now, some breakfast. He was famished.

o o o

Will Hawkins was at his best in front of a crowd. For a Sunday morning campaign stop in Austin, the throng of three thousand faithful supporters was considered by most political pundits to be absolutely massive. Senator Hawkins was not one to miss an opportunity. As he extolled the virtues of his policies, with the economy, drug enforcement, and the environment getting most of the attention, the crowd cheered endlessly.

His staff was waiting in the wings, watching with pride as Will ended his rousing speech with a stirring quote: "If I am elected president, I assure you that I will not sleep until we've amputated the hands that feed drugs to our children."

The crowd roared as Will stepped down from the podium.

As Ian had predicted, Will's next move was to approach the crowd that was chanting, "Hawkins, Hawkins, Hawkins." Ian's plan was perfect, and he was prepared, having dreamt of this confrontational moment for a long time. As the senator inched toward the rail where he had been pressed by the surging crowd, Ian coolly revealed the sign he had carefully created the night before. It wasn't long before one of Hawkins's staff spotted the sign reading, "The Hawkins Administration will change the world" and began subtly moving Will in that direction. As Will approached, Ian took the note from his pants pocket, ready to slip it to the senator. The moment had finally arrived. Will Hawkins locked eyes with the sign-wielding supporter, recognizing the momentary sensation that they had somehow met previously. But before he could ask the question, the two men were shaking hands, and Will realized the man had slipped him a note.

Ian leaned toward Will ever so slightly and said, "I think you'd prefer to read that later. And I'm quite sure you'll find it interesting."

Will looked at the man with the British accent, intrigued at his brashness. But just as quickly as it happened, Will shrugged, put the note in his pocket, and moved on. Ian smiled to himself and worked his way through the crowd back toward the Driskill.

∘ ∘ ∘

The four Mexican Nationals, who just days earlier had crossed the US-Mexico border with enough firepower to conquer a third-world nation, now sat in a small, clean motel room in Glenwood Springs, Colorado, biding their time until evening. And what an evening it would be. This day marked the beginning of the ecological reign of terror envisioned by Sen. Will Hawkins and executed by the ruthless criminal network of Carlos Pendrill. In the minds of the terrorists, the clock was moving at a snail's pace. It felt as if 9:00 p.m. would never arrive. This was the moment they had trained for around the clock for the past several weeks.

The plan was complete and impeccably detailed; all that was left was the waiting. At approximately 9:00 p.m., the truck carrying toxic waste from the mining site in Utah would pass through Glenwood Springs on its way to a disposal site in Northern New Mexico. It was a relatively simple mission. When the truck stopped at the weigh station in Glenwood Springs just prior to entering the famed Glenwood Canyon, it would be delayed by a well-compensated attendant. During the delay, two of Pendrill's henchmen would sneak under the truck and attach a small device to the right front tire. The device, a plastic explosive with remote detonation capability, was designed to separate the front wheel and tire from the axle, causing the truck to severely lurch to the right in a canyon that left little room for driver error.

By 8:40 the terrorists were on the move. As they pulled to within visual range of the weigh station, they shut off the headlights. The two men in the back silently exited the car and disappeared into the darkness. At 8:57 the truck with a full load of toxic waste pulled into the station, just as they had planned. Fifteen minutes later, without a single contingency plan requiring execution, the two terrorists returned to their vehicle. Phase I of their plan had been completed; now it was time to wait.

Ten minutes later the semi left the weigh station heading east on I-70 into Glenwood Canyon. The terrorists followed approximately a half-mile behind. The timing of the plan was extremely tight, and flawless execution was mandatory. The woman in the front passenger seat was calculating the truck's speed and the timing at which it would be in the detonation zone.

The group only had a three-second window to detonate and ensure maximum effectiveness. "Forty-five seconds," the woman spoke in perfect English. The man sitting directly behind the woman held the remote detonator softly, with his thumb poised above the detonate button. She began her countdown. "Ten, nine, eight, seven," as the man waited for the word fire. At the split second that she spoke the first syllable, the man pushed the button. The small explosion was immediate and highly visible, even from a half mile back. What happened next seemed to take an eternity. The truck lurched right, then the tank began to swing back and forth, causing all four terrorists to hold their collective breath. Just as the truck appeared to be slowing and not sliding toward the steep embankment that led to the river, the tank flipped and flew over the guardrail, dragging the cab with it. The entire truck rolled two more times and landed squarely on some large boulders at the bank of the Colorado River, splitting the tank and spilling its poisonous contents into the longest river west of the Continental Divide.

The terrorists grinned with the satisfaction of a job well done. Little did they know or care that within an hour, half the country would be appalled by the tragedy and searching for someone to blame it on. All they knew was that Phase I of a four-phase process had been successfully completed. Their boss would be pleased.

# thirty-three

The Monday morning meeting in Will Hawkins's office had all the ingredients of a national crisis: phones ringing, multiple newscasts playing on the wall of TVs, advisers running in with updates, and the candidate's top adviser, John Rollins, sitting across the desk from him as he took a call from the leader of arguably the most powerful special interest group in the country.

As David Ellis and Will Hawkins discussed the environmental tragedy of the previous evening, Will explained his position on the situation. "David, I am as appalled as you are. The fact that we would ever allow toxic waste to travel a route along one of our most cherished waterways is a travesty. And I'm here to tell you, if I'm elected president, protection of the environment will be one of my top priorities."

"Senator," Ellis said, his voice trembling with emotion, "I believe you. That is why I've committed my support to you. You have my pledge that the foundation will provide unprecedented resources to your candidacy."

Will, smiling from ear to ear, interrupted Ellis, "David, you will not regret this. Our partnership, and I use that term purposely, will make a mark on the environment that will change our children's future."

Ellis responded, "I'm with you, Senator. And as soon as we hang up, I will be arranging a news conference that will formally announce The Future State Foundation's support of Senator William S. Hawkins for president of the United States."

"Thank you, David. Let's talk soon." As Will hung up, he looked at John Rollins and smiled, "Well, at least something is going right."

"Well, it's a start," Rollins responded, "because we've got a real problem here with your long-lost friend from London. We've done some digging. His name is Ian McKay, and he is a Special Ops expert with the British Military."

The room went quiet as Will pondered the situation. After moments of silence, Will spoke as if he were thinking out loud. "It seems that the appropriate next step would be to arrange for our friend Mr. McKay to accompany us to Colorado where we could quietly discuss the situation and then dispose of him with little or no interference."

"You've got to be kidding me!" Rollins exclaimed. "This whole thing is getting way out of hand." The two men sat in silence, and then John Rollins asked, "Have you ever heard of a labyrinth?"

Will responded coldly, "Of course, what do you think I am, an idiot?"

"No, but I've got to tell you that's exactly what we're creating here. Each time we enter into another illegal activity, the odds of everything working out as we planned exponentially decrease. We've got to clean up what has already been initiated and get ourselves out of this downward spiral."

Will silently stared at Rollins, showing absolutely no emotion, so Rollins continued.

"It reminds me of a family vacation when I was twelve. We were driving in Northern California and went to visit the Winchester Mystery House. Old Lady Winchester was the heiress to the firearm fortune and had obviously lived life being a few cards short of a full deck. Over many years, she had created this grand mansion where she planned to live out her years. The problem was she was never satisfied with the final product. So she continually added wings and rooms and staircases with no master plan in mind. The result was rooms with no windows, staircases running into walls, and a general layout of a home with no semblance of order."

"John, I hate to interrupt this compelling story, but where are you going with this? I've got a full day ahead of me."

"Where I'm going with this is that that's when my father taught me the valuable lesson of the labyrinth. He explained that in life, just like building a structure, a master plan is required. I don't believe we currently have a master plan. Therefore, by default, we are creating a labyrinth that I'm not sure we will escape."

Once again, while looking interested, Will stared at John Rollins in silence. While some of Rollins's diatribe made sense, Will was thinking to himself that regardless of the risk, he could not afford to have a blackmailer around who knew he had killed someone in an alley behind a bar more than two decades ago. It didn't matter that less than twenty-four hours earlier, he himself hadn't known the unfortunate outcome of that fateful night. After more silence, Will finally spoke.

"Okay, then, it's settled; we'll take Mr. McKay to Colorado and make sure he's never heard from again."

Rollins nodded disgustedly, knowing that any further discussion was futile. He was in too deep to get out and at a disadvantage regarding influence. "Well, we're going to have to be very careful, because another guest will also be traveling with us to Colorado."

"And who might that be?"

"Greg Larson. This is our opportunity to get Pulitzer-caliber coverage from a 'skeptical convert' in the press."

"Perfect! I'll be happy to give Larson and the nation's press an interview that will swing our great nation's voters."

○ ○ ○

Jack McCarthy and Kate Anson entered Denver International Airport with the intention of getting a rental car. They parked the Lincoln Town Car on Level 3 of the west parking structure with no intention of ever going near it again. Their plan was relatively simple but also extremely risky. As they boarded the bus that would shuttle them to the Budget Rental Car counter, they nervously held each other's hands, posing as a tourist couple. Their next steps had been scripted on the nearly thirteen-hour drive from Dallas to Denver.

Once they rented any available SUV using Jack's credit card, they would look for their unwitting accomplice. The plan was to identify a young man traveling alone who might be willing to trade his just-rented subcompact for their more luxurious SUV. The story they had concocted would center around Kate's ex-boyfriend. They would explain to their target that the ex was very wealthy and very jealous and had reason to believe they were headed to Colorado. If he was willing to trade, not only would they pay for both cars, but would also give him $100 for his trouble. It would take the right individual to make this work, but they hadn't come up with anything better. And they knew that once they used one of their credit cards, all pursuit would center on Colorado.

As Jack and Kate entered the rental-car building, the first thing they noticed was that it was packed. They smiled at each other, thinking that finding someone willing to trade vehicles had just gotten easier. Jack was scanning the room looking for unwitting targets when the nearby newspaper stand caught his eye. There it was in bold type on the front page of *The Denver Morning News*: "COLORADO RIVER TRAGEDY."

Jack nearly vomited. He quickly dug out some change and grabbed a paper from the dispenser. He couldn't believe what he was reading: toxic waste in the Colorado River . . . and he had known it was going to happen. Seconds later, he heard a gasp from behind him. Kate had just read the headline over his shoulder.

"My God, what's happening here?" Kate exclaimed quietly.

"It's our worst nightmare," groaned Jack. "They're actually following through on this madness."

"What do we do now?" Kate said.

"We stick with the plan. It's more imperative than ever that we get to the president. And he's only a two-hour drive away."

They quickly got into line, ready to attack the next and most improbable leg of their journey. As the woman behind the counter handed them their keys, she asked if they needed a map. Jack quickly said no as they headed for the front lobby to find their target.

It wasn't easy. The first two guys they approached emphatically declined. The second actually added a "fuck off" when they persisted. But as was usual in bizarre situations, the third time was somehow a charm. The young man was clearly hesitant at first but clearly loosened when the offer was raised to $300 cash and a free rental car. The two parties agreed that the young man would just insert his keys in the slot when returning so that a receipt would be mailed to Jack. Jack in turn promised to charge the man's bill to his credit card upon return, explaining that he was paying for his buddy's rental. The returns would happen on Thursday, the day the young man was to return to Kansas City. Jack added for assurance that the man should call Budget on Thursday evening, and if everything was not copasetic, he could explain the situation to the rental car company and report the vehicle as stolen.

The man looked around as any suspicious character would, but nobody seemed to care. The keys and cash were quickly exchanged, and the man walked off with a slight spring in his step.

Jack and Kate found their Ford Fusion. "Is it just me, or do all rentals look alike?" Jack asked rhetorically. And off they went.

As Jack and Kate merged on to I-70 from Peña Blvd, Jack blurted out, "We've got to get to Hughes and end this nightmare."

His fatigue clearly showing, he was referencing a meeting with the president as if it were already scheduled.

# thirty-four

The phone in room 720 of the Four Seasons Hotel in Austin rang twice. Ian McKay snatched the phone from its cradle as he re-entered his room from the balcony overlooking Lake Austin. "Hello."

"Sir, this is a representative for Senator Will Hawkins. Have I reached the right room?"

"Yes."

"Sir, we have discussed the terms of your proposal, and Senator Hawkins has agreed, in principle, assuming certain conditions are met."

"Listen," Ian said, "I am not here to negotiate. The terms of my proposal are nonnegotiable, and if they are not acceptable to the senator, then I will go to the press. End of story."

"Whoa, hold on there, sir. These conditions are actually quite minor. They are simply designed to ensure that there is no trail that links any of this unfortunate transaction back to the senator."

"Listen, you fucking political lackey, the unfortunate part of this transaction happened a long time ago, and you have no idea the heartache and hardship it has caused. But go on, I'm listening."

"The senator does not wish for this meeting to happen anywhere in Texas. The publicity and scrutiny surrounding his campaign, coupled with the shock of your initial contact, has him, as you might expect, slightly paranoid."

"Continue," McKay responded, slightly relieved.

"The senator is suggesting instead that you meet him in Colorado this Thursday. He's taking a little retreat to his family home in Vail, and the press has purposely not been made aware of this trip. It is also imperative that you get to Denver International Airport on Thursday by noon without leaving a trail of how you got there."

"Now, how do you expect me to do that?" Ian asked, clearly irritated.

"Well," the representative said, slightly sarcastically, "you could fly. You could drive. You could take a bus. There are many transportation options in this great country of ours."

"Fuck you! I know how to get there; the question is how to get there without using my own name," Ian blurted out, knowing his documents could never be traced back to him.

"That sounds like a personal problem, sir. I'm just the messenger. Now, once you make it to the Denver airport on Thursday, you'll see a large piece of artwork in the middle of the main terminal, a colorful map of the United States. One of our representatives will meet you there. After verifying that you made it to Denver without leaving a trail, this person will accompany you to Vail where you will meet with Senator Hawkins. After completion of your requested meeting with the senator, the package you're expecting will be transferred, and someone will escort you back to Denver. Once this portion of your journey is complete, we will drop you at a downtown location of your choice. That is the last time anyone associated with Senator Hawkins will expect to see or hear from you. Ever.

"Now, just to ensure compliance, Mr. McKay, some of our people have done a little research in the news archives and public records in London. We know where your niece lives; we know where your mother lives; we know every friend and family member you have in the UK. Please don't put us in a position of needing to use that information."

"Are you threatening me?" Ian asked, already knowing the answer.

"No, sir, just communicating that we believe there is recourse. It's kind of like buying insurance."

Ian had always suspected, in the back of his mind, that a determined searcher might identify him through the circumstances surrounding his brother's death. This change of plans was far from optimal, but he quickly assessed that it posed no greater risk than the rendezvous he had actually proposed. And now there were Patricia and Lizzie to consider.

"I'll see you in Colorado," he muttered, finally.

Ian heard the click on the end of the other line and knew the conversation was over. While infuriated by the threats, he smiled to himself, believing that he was one step closer to his objective.

o o o

Greg Larson was sitting in his favorite leather chair sipping a cold Coors Light, flipping through the channels mindlessly, when the phone rang. He quickly grabbed his cell phone off the coffee table, expecting to hear from John Sterling, the researcher he'd been waiting for his entire career.

"Hello."

"Greg, this is John Rollins, chief of staff for the Will Hawkins presidential campaign."

Larson immediately sat up in his chair, thinking to himself, No shit, everyone in town knows who John Rollins is. "Yes, Mr. Rollins. What can I do for you?"

"You can start by calling me John. But more important is what you can do for me and the Will Hawkins presidential campaign."

"And what might that be?"

"After significant discussion throughout the senior ranks of the campaign, we've come to the conclusion that you are the perfect person to do an exclusive interview series with Senator Hawkins."

Inside, Larson's excitement could barely be contained. But, he knew it was imperative that he stay cool. "Go on, John. I'm listening."

"Well, that's really the headline, Greg. We've been following your *Free Press* series on the senator, and based on everything we've seen, you appear to be the perfect person to inform the world about the political platform that will lead this country to a new level of economic and ecological prosperity."

The hair on the back of Larson's neck stood on end as he listened to Rollins's bullshit. "I've got to tell you, John, I've never been so offended. I am nobody's puppet. And if you think I'm going to be led to a preconceived conclusion by you and your fucking campaign, you are sorely mistaken."

"Greg, you are a Pulitzer Prize winner. I never intended to imply a specific slant on your story. It's just that everything we've seen from you so far has been so positive."

"Well, to tell you the truth, that's all I've found. If there was anything negative that came up in my research, I would have told that side of the story as well. And having said that, as long as you understand that I write stories based on facts and what I believe the general public wants or needs to know, then I'd be honored to have an exclusive interview with the future president of the United States." Larson smiled to himself as he continued the sales pitch. "I believe in Senator Hawkins's platforms and would walk across a mile of broken glass to spend some one-on-one time with him, regardless of the chance to publish a series of stories."

"Fantastic!" Rollins exclaimed. "That's what I was hoping to hear. Now here's what we'd like to propose. Thursday morning at 8:00 a.m., Senator Hawkins's private jet will be leaving Love Field headed to Eagle County Airport in Colorado. The senator is planning to spend a few quiet days in the mountains to get some much-needed rest. We'd like you to accompany us on the trip. It should give you an inside look at the senator, his staff, and the inner workings of his campaign. Now, the senator is admittedly wound up pretty tight. So the interview process can't begin until Saturday morning. So, if your schedule doesn't allow a Thursday departure, then we can arrange for you to arrive Friday evening as an alternative."

"No, no," Larson quickly responded. "I wouldn't miss this opportunity for the world."

"Great, then plan on being at Hangar 7 on the private-jet side of Love Field around 7:30 Thursday morning. It's just off Mockingbird and Lemmon. You'll see the entrance."

"Got it," Larson responded. "Looking forward to it."

"As are we," Rollins said. "Goodbye."

○ ○ ○

As Rollins hung up the phone, he smiled to himself. Finally, something that had gone according to plan.

○ ○ ○

Greg Larson also was smiling to himself. His plan, too, was taking shape. An exclusive interview with the front-running Democratic candidate coupled with exclusive information that would change the face of the upcoming election. Larson couldn't help but think once more about how interesting it was going to be to see Will Hawkins's reaction when he asked him about his relationship with Carlos Pendrill. Then, before he had time to recover, he'd hit him again with a question surrounding his relationship with Jack McCarthy, his fugitive aide. An ex-roommate who was the world's most notorious drug trafficker, an ex-aide implicated in drug trafficking, the murder of the aide's girlfriend, and a shooting outside the Dallas Police Department . . . this truly was going to be an interview to remember.

# thirty-five

Doug Flannery, the deputy director of South Carolina's Charleston Nuclear Facility, had just pulled into a dingy Motel 6 approximately thirty miles from the power plant. Flannery had been approached the night before at the Roadkill Bar, where he often stopped for a beer after work. The handsome, articulate Hispanic man who had approached him suggested that they meet regarding an opportunity to make an astronomical sum of money. After agonizing most of the night, Flannery decided to hear the man out. He knew whatever the opportunity was, to make big money, it had to do with his place of employment, and it had to be illegal. But he rationalized to himself that whatever it was, his employer deserved it. He had recently been passed over for a promotion to director of the facility, and he was still bitter.

Flannery knocked on the door of room 112 and was promptly greeted by the man he had met the night before. There were two other men and a woman also in the room. Flannery shuddered as he suddenly realized that he could be in significant danger. His fears, however, were quickly diminished as the man assured him there was nothing to worry about and motioned him toward a makeshift work space in the corner of the room. Two of the men sat down with him at the table. The other man and the woman looked on with interest, sitting on the edge of the double bed.

"Mr. Flannery, can we get you anything to drink?" asked his acquaintance from the previous evening.

"I'd love a beer if you have one," Flannery replied.

With one nod from the leader, the man sitting on the bed went to the cooler under the sink and brought Flannery a bottle.

"Thanks," Flannery said, nodding to the man. "Now, what do you fine people have on your mind?"

"Well," the leader began, "it's really quite simple. We've been asked to create a situation at your facility, and after extensive research, we found that you might be a person who would be willing to help us."

Flannery bristled at the arrogance in the man's voice. "One, what makes you think I'd help? Two, what research led you to this conclusion? And three, what the fuck do you mean by 'a situation'?"

"Calm down, Mr. Flannery. This is an opportunity, not an inquisition. We are simply proposing a mutually beneficial partnership. As for why you've been identified as a candidate for this partnership, you've spent the last three weeks at the Roadkill Bar bad-mouthing your employer for passing you over for a promotion. We simply happened to have been in the right place at the right time and overheard some of what you had to say."

Flannery took a deep breath and nodded. "Okay, what do you have in mind?"

"Well," the leader responded, "we've been retained to create a minor meltdown at a US nuclear facility. We've chosen your facility for its rural location, hoping to minimize any long-term damage to the environment and any significant impact on the local population."

Flannery's mouth gaped open. "You want to create a minor meltdown? There's no such thing! Any meltdown is catastrophic. You must be fucking crazy." Flannery started to get up, but the other man at the table put a powerful hand on his shoulder, easing him back into his chair.

"Don't be so hasty, Mr. Flannery," the leader continued. "For your help in this endeavor we are prepared to pay you $250,000."

Flannery sagged in his chair. He didn't know what to say. Part of him couldn't believe the luck of being included. The other part of him knew that, should he participate, it would be one of the most infamous terrorist acts in American history. The room was silent. Finally, the terrorist leader spoke.

"The plan is quite simple. We will provide you a very ingenious incendiary device. This device will have remote detonation capability, and, once detonated, it will spill a very powerful acid compound that will ultimately eat through any metallic material in its way. Now if our information is correct . . . " While the terrorist leader continued to explain, he nodded to his partner across the table who then unfolded a very detailed blueprint of the nuclear facility.

"How did you get this document?" Flannery asked in amazement. "This blueprint is classified level 4. You must know someone in some very influential circles."

The leader ignored the interruption. "We believe if the device is placed right here," the leader pointed with his index finger, "sometime between three and four hours later, the acid will melt right through the system to the core. And, well, Mr. Flannery . . . you know the rest of the story better than we do."

Flannery stared at the blueprint in silence. $250,000 tax-free . . . That would be a pretty good trade for getting passed over for promotion by those SOBs . . .

He mumbled, "Can I sleep on it?"

"I'm sorry, but no. Our timeline is very tight, and if we've misread your unhappiness with your employer, then we'll have to go to Plan B."

The tone of the voice used by the leader sent shivers down Flannery's spine, and the silence that ensued seemed like an eternity. Finally Flannery whispered, "I'm in."

The lead terrorist spent the next ten minutes explaining the simple plan in detail. He finished by explaining how the transfer of money would take place and how Flannery would meet them in the same room one hour after the accident first made the news. The account number, account password, and other relevant documents would be handed off with the expectation that they would never see or hear from him again. Flannery said he understood.

The woman terrorist who had barely been noticed throughout the discussion came forward. She laid the incendiary device on the card table, and in the next two minutes, she very efficiently and effectively explained the placement of the device. When she was finished, Flannery left without another word.

o o o

David Ellis took the stage at the National Conference for The Future State Foundation. The 1,500 or so foundation faithful had arrived at Exhibit Hall J of the San Francisco Convention Center nearly two hours earlier. After a reception where the wine and beer were flowing freely and Ellis had pulled a no-show, the throng of fervent supporters was primed to hear from their charismatic leader.

As the cheers rang out for more than a minute, Ellis continually raised his hands over his head, trying to quiet the crowd. Finally, a break in the roar allowed him to begin. "Ladies and gentlemen, thank you all for being here. First, I must apologize for not attending the reception earlier this evening. Two days ago, my intention was to spend time with all of you, the greatest political movement this country has seen since the civil rights marches of the 1960s."

With that, the crowd erupted again. Another break allowed him to continue. "As I was saying, my original goal was to spend time with all of you, but that was before the travesty that took place in Colorado just forty-eight hours ago. This tragedy, and I don't use that term lightly, changed the face of ecological politics forever. The foundation, a result of our collective passion for the future of this country, has known for some time that an accident of this type was just around the corner. Our current administration has ignored us. And they have ignored our children's opportunity for a better future."

Again the crowd applauded, but this time with stoic determination, not the exhilaration that had been exhibited just moments earlier.

Ellis continued, "We, the people of this country, must take charge of our future. While ecology is the foundation of our mission, we must continue to endorse a broader agenda.

"At the same time that a reduction of our budget deficit has taken place and our friends in Washington argue over who should get the credit, that same budget deficit alone continues to rival the annual economy of most countries in the free world. While our leaders fight to take credit for putting more police on the street and raising the annual salaries of our children's teachers, violent crime and drug use proliferate, and the educational measures for math and reading continue to erode. Our nation is not better off than it was ten years ago, contrary to what past administrations have claimed. Our nation is on the brink of some of the greatest challenges the new millennium has to offer."

Ellis's speech continued for another twenty-five minutes with a raucous interruption from his supporters almost every ninety seconds.

"Now, before we adjourn, I think it is important to set the tone for the foundation as we attack the next twelve months. That's why I have chosen to personally endorse Senator William S. Hawkins for the presidency of the United States, and I'd like your support to provide the foundation's endorsement as well."

Ellis's supporters erupted just as he hoped they would. Most of them had privately supported Hawkins for months but were waiting for their beloved leader's endorsement to publicly begin their push. Now they had it.

# thirty-six

As Jack McCarthy and Kate Anson drove their bartered Ford over Vail Pass, the realization hit that they had no idea where they would stay. Vail was a resort town, the president and his entourage arrived tomorrow, and the inability to use a credit card made the simple task of getting a room somewhat formidable.

They were driving in silence, contemplating their plight, when Jack finally spoke. "There's a central reservations number in Vail that should help us figure out who has rooms available."

"But how do we check in without a credit card? Isn't that the usual requirement?"

"Of course it is, but we know that's not an option, so we're going to have to get creative."

Kate thought for a moment and then said, "We'll just tell them our luggage was lost and our credit cards were inside. We'll say that we expect delivery from American Airlines tomorrow or the next day, but until then we'll use cash as our deposit. We don't look like vagrants or anything; maybe they'll go for it."

Jack shrugged his shoulders and said, "What do we have to lose?"

Jack wheeled the car into the public parking lot at the edge of Vail Village and found a spot. On the top floor of the parking structure, they found a pay phone and called the central reservation number. As it turned out, rooms were plentiful in Vail. After a lengthy deliberation, they decided on the Sonnenalp Hotel in the heart of the village. Their rationale was that as one of the nicest places in town, the hotel would be helpful and understanding toward someone with missing luggage and plenty of cash.

As it turned out, they were correct. With a $500 cash deposit and an agreement to check back with the manager in forty-eight hours, Jack and Kate had a luxurious room overlooking Gore Creek.

"This place is beautiful," Kate said with a hint of girlishness in her voice.

"Yes, it is. I just wish my first chance to stay here was under different circumstances." Oh shit, Jack thought, wondering if his comment might have somehow hurt Kate's feelings.

"Tell me about it," Kate said, allaying his concerns. "Now, how are we going to get to the president?"

At the end of an hour of brainstorming, they had a game plan—a weak one, but it was the best they could do on short notice. Simplicity seemed to be the best approach. Once the president and his entourage arrived, Jack and Kate would wait for the right moment and approach a Secret Service agent with a note. The contents of the note would outline everything that had transpired.

They were counting on the fact that President Hughes's son had gone to the University of Colorado at the same time as Jack. Though they had been only acquaintances twenty years earlier, Jack had stayed in touch with Bill Farmer, who was still quite close with Hughes's son. The story for the Secret Service would be that Farmer was also in Vail with his fiancée and would love a chance to visit the president if he had a moment. The contents of the note had their Sonnenalp contact information. Jack's biggest fear was being recognized before gaining access to the president, but it was a chance they were going to have to take.

With the note written and more than twelve hours until the president and his entourage were to arrive, Jack and Kate decided to relax and spend an evening in the quaint village. Step one was to buy some clean clothes, so they wandered through the village visiting the type of stores one might expect to find on Fifth Avenue in Manhattan.

"This feels like a dream," Kate said excitedly. "It's a mix between an alpine village and a mall in Dallas."

"Pretty amazing, isn't it?" Jack responded. "All you need here is time and money."

After making purchases at Ralph Lauren's Polo store and Gorsuch, a high-end, alpine Neiman's, the two returned to their room to clean up. Jack showered and changed quickly and turned the bathroom over to Kate. Thirty minutes later she emerged, and Jack turned to see one of the most stunning women he'd ever set eyes on.

"Wow, you look great," he said with a surprised tone.

"I know it's shocking, but I do get dressed up once in a while," Kate said, laughing. "Let's go, I'm starving."

The couple wandered out into the village in search of a restaurant. Within minutes they had a table at a place that looked both quiet and somewhat private. The service was impeccable, the food and wine exquisite. For nearly two hours, Jack and Kate forgot about their current lot in life and enjoyed each other's company immensely. When the check arrived, Jack quickly plunked down three $100 bills, and they wandered back out into the village. The streets were relatively quiet, and Jack led Kate past the fountain plaza and down some stairs to a small parklike area adjacent to Gore Creek. As they strolled toward the pedestrian bridge, Kate stopped to look in the window of a shoe store that had closed hours earlier.

Jack walked up beside her and said, "Didn't you get enough shopping earlier today?"

"A girl can never have too many shoes, Jack. You should know that."

They both laughed, turning toward one another. Without another word, they leaned in toward one another and kissed, very gently at first, and then with more passion, as the isolation, anxiety, and loneliness of the past days thrust them into an emotional storm that made the moment all the more intense.

When the kiss ended, Jack took Kate by the hand, and they strode silently back to the hotel. As they entered the room, an awkward feeling told each of them that this was neither the time nor the place to begin an intimate relationship. They both wanted to, but the events of the past few days that had brought them together were not the foundation of a lasting relationship, or any type of intimate relationship for that matter.

Without a word, Jack grabbed the remote control and flipped on the TV. Channel 9 was a Denver-area affiliate, and the 10:00 news was just beginning. Both Jack and Kate were barely listening, contemplating how to let each other down easily. Those thoughts came to an abrupt halt when the male anchor introduced the top story of the night: an explosion in the parking lot of a downtown Denver hotel.

"A car rented to Jack McCarthy, alleged drug trafficker and former staff member of Senator William S. Hawkins's presidential campaign, was been completely destroyed, presumably with him in it."

"Oh, my God!" Kate cried as they rushed toward one another. As they embraced, she trembled. "We killed him. It was our fault."

"We did," Jack replied coldly. He would have at least expected Hawkins's people to verify it was him before rigging the car. Beneath the fear summoned by the vicious act, Jack felt a layer of absolute determination. *Hawkins, you fuck, I'm taking you down.*

# thirty-seven

Greg Larson drove his Jeep Grand Cherokee down Lemmon Avenue toward Love Field. As he veered right, crossing Mockingbird onto Marsh Lane, he spotted a number of private jets and finally saw the entrance to the private terminal. He parked his car in a guest space and entered the small building located at the far east side of the airport grounds. Upon entering, Greg was greeted by a man in a black suit, a black tie, and a white shirt with sunglasses hanging around his neck. The prototypical security guy, Greg thought to himself.

The agent clone spoke first. "Greg Larson, I presume?"

"Dr. Stanley," Greg joked, unable to help himself.

When the man did not react, Greg wondered if he had blown the famous line uttered more than a century ago in Africa. Before he had time to question himself further, the man continued.

"Sir, if you don't mind, I'd like to have a quick check of your bags."

"No problem, I fully expected it."

The bodyguard thoroughly examined both Greg's briefcase and his duffel bag. When he was through, he ran each bag through an x-ray machine as a double check.

"Sir, you're the first one here, but you're free to board whenever you like."

The bodyguard escorted Greg out onto the tarmac. As they approached what appeared to be a commercial airliner, Greg realized and kicked himself for expecting that he was riding to Colorado on an ordinary private jet. This plane looked like a custom 737, and he couldn't wait to check it out. He ascended the stairway to the entrance of the jet and was greeted by a male flight attendant whose nametag read "Rick."

"Mr. Larson, welcome aboard. Our scheduled departure is in twenty-five minutes. Senator Hawkins and his team should be arriving shortly. Let me show you to your seat."

The two men entered the plane, passing the cockpit on the left, then went through a short hallway and into the main salon. Greg was in awe. He had never seen anything remotely like this, and they were only in the main cabin. Rick mentioned that the private quarters were in the rear portion of the plane.

"Wow," Greg said quietly. "It's like a tour bus on steroids."

"It is pretty amazing," Rick responded. "But you get used to it."

As the two men walked down the aisle, Greg was checking out everything. The main cabin had separate seating areas with what appeared to be mahogany walls separating them. Each area was appointed with leather couches, leather chairs with accompanying ottomans, coffee tables with built-in phones, laptops, and scanners, and a wall of four televisions designated London, New York, Dallas, and Tokyo. The second "den," as Rick referred to it, was where Greg was supposed to sit.

"Pick any seat," Rick instructed. "This flight will be relatively empty."

Greg chose the chair next to the window and settled in. As he stared out the window, he contemplated his interview strategy. How would he confront Will Hawkins? What would the senator's response be? As the moment arrived, would Greg have the wherewithal to go the distance? All of these questions nagged at him as he noticed three Lincoln Town Cars pull into the parking lot. His heart started to race as Senator Will Hawkins and his entourage exited the vehicles.

Then the adrenaline rush hit him. This was the moment he had waited for since his last Pulitzer. At that very moment, he knew with

100 percent conviction that he was going to nail Will Hawkins's ass to the wall.

Nevertheless, as Greg watched the entourage confidently cross the tarmac, a sick feeling hit him square in the gut. They were so confident, almost cocky. It appeared to be the Camelot of the next millennium. He couldn't help a slight feeling of awe. He fervently wished for another time in history that represented hope. But he knew in his heart that Senator Hawkins was a fraud—very polished and a fabulous speaker—but without a shred of sincerity.

The entourage entered the plane. Hawkins was not in front, as Greg had expected. Instead, three men, almost clones of the man who had first met him in the terminal, entered first. It was obvious they were trained bodyguards. When they were satisfied there was no threat, Senator Hawkins strode in. Greg was surprised at his presence: handsome, smiling, clearly in control. Will Hawkins could have just as easily been entering a crowded auditorium. His gait was fast and deliberate, and he walked straight toward Greg.

"Greg, I can't tell you how excited I am to have you with us on this trip. A journalist of your reputation covering my campaign is an honor and a huge opportunity. Now, having said that, it's only a bonus if your coverage is favorable."

Greg started to interrupt with a reporter's obligatory no-guarantees speech, but Hawkins continued before he had a chance.

"Of course, there are no guarantees. But I do believe you are innately fair, and I am confident that the facts will speak for themselves."

Greg was thinking to himself what a surprise was in store for Hawkins and his staff. The two men continued their chat for nearly five minutes, covering topics ranging from fly-fishing in Colorado to Hawkins's stance on a range of public policies. At an appropriate breaking point, Will Hawkins excused himself to visit with other guests and finally adjourned to the back cabin that had a private bedroom and study.

On cue, a female flight attendant, who could have easily passed for a Dallas Cowboys cheerleader, asked Greg what he would like to eat and drink during their flight. While the cuisine sounded delicious by any standard, he passed on the food and ordered a double Grey Goose on the rocks, then reclined, settling in for the two-hour flight. As the plane lifted off the runway at Love Field, Greg couldn't help smiling. He knew he was on his way to the most explosive interview of his career.

o o o

Ian McKay was standing next to the US map artwork in Denver International Airport described to him two days prior. As he scanned the crowd, waiting for his contact, he couldn't help but wonder how he'd gotten to this point in such a short amount of time. Everything had happened so quickly that his normal, methodical approach to planning had been marginalized. At that moment, Ian realized he had no definitive contingency plan and had not made any arrangements should he not return home to England. He was actually contemplating walking away when he spotted the men he was looking for. They were dressed in black suits, white shirts, and black ties, and both had sunglasses dangling around their necks.

They walked right up to Ian, and one man said, "Do, re, mi."

Ian responded with the agreed response from the song in *The Sound of Music*: "Fa, so, la."

The man asked quietly, "May I see your ticket stub, please?"

It struck Ian as funny. He sounded just like a ticket agent at the gate. Ian laughed and said, "I don't have a ticket."

The two men looked at each other, frustrated. "Mr. McKay, you had explicit instructions to reach Denver International Airport anonymously. Exactly how did you get here?"

"I drove."

"Sir, this is a violation of our agreement. You were explicitly told not to rent a car."

"I didn't. I bought a very used Honda Accord from a sleazy used-car dealer who didn't seem to care that my name was Tom Cruise."

The two men smiled as Ian handed them the bill of sale from College Motors with the buyer name of Tom Cruise.

"Follow us." They turned and walked toward the west exit of the airport.

Once Ian was settled in the back of the customized Chevy Suburban, the second man, who was in the front passenger seat, turned and began the lengthy instruction phase during the two-hour drive to Vail. Ian was going to be staying in the guest quarters of the Hawkins family estate. It was imperative that no one see him during his entire stay in Vail. He was to stay away from all windows, and tomorrow morning at exactly 8:00 a.m., they would bring Senator Hawkins to him. Their expectation was that the meeting should take no more than ten minutes. The senator would bring a large, nondescript duffel bag with the agreed amount of money.

Ian's mind wandered. What was he thinking? He felt as if he were walking into a lion's den. But he rationalized that Hawkins wasn't crazy. Paying the ransom was the prudent, easy thing to do.

"Mr. McKay," the man interrupted his thoughts. "Do you understand?"

"I'm sorry," Ian responded. "Could you go over that last part again?"

"I said, once the transaction is completed, we will drive you back to DIA, and we don't expect to ever hear from you again."

Ian nodded, and the rest of the trip passed in silence.

# thirty-eight

Jack and Kate were positioned at side-by-side windows in their room overlooking the quaint chapel across the street. They hadn't left their positions for well over an hour. President Hughes was staying right up the street at a stone mansion once owned by the Webster family of dictionary fame, and it was imperative that they know when the president and his entourage decided to visit town. Their plan was predicated on being there as the president strolled through town so that they could identify a Secret Service agent on the periphery who was isolated and therefore approachable.

Jack had spent hours crafting the note they hoped would reach the president. It was well thought out, with enough proprietary information to provide some level of authenticity to the many eyes that were sure to scrutinize it. But the content of the note was irrelevant if the initial approach was not flawless.

The plan was simple: Jack and Kate would both approach an outlying Secret Service agent and explain that Jack had attended college with the president's son and was hoping to get a brief chance to say hello. Kate was the diversion. They hoped that with the appropriate attire and a disarming smile, she would be able to preoccupy the agent just enough to take the note and pass it along to his superiors later.

About twenty minutes later, movement up the street got their attention. Four men, casually dressed but looking out of place, were slowly moving down the street, scanning up, down, and side-to-side. It was clear that the larger entourage would be along shortly.

Jack and Kate jumped back from their positions; being observed looking out the window would be a dead giveaway. Within a minute, they both were prepared to exit the hotel. By the time they reached the lobby, the president and his team were passing the valet entrance of the hotel, about to take a right toward the heart of the village.

Jack and Kate stood still, watching along with the rest of the tourists and locals who had noticed the commotion. Once the main group had rounded the corner, the twosome began scanning the street for an agent bringing up the rear. It turned out to be quite simple, as four more agents brought up the rear. After watching for no more than ten seconds, the choice was obvious: The young agent closest to them, though doing his job, was obviously spending an inordinate amount of time observing Kate.

Once the rear escort team had passed, Jack and Kate casually followed. For the next five minutes, they were just two tourists window-shopping at all the fine establishments Vail had to offer but always keeping their Secret Service target in view. When the president finally entered a store and the various agents took their positions, they knew this was their chance. They approached the target together, Jack speaking first. "Excuse me, I know this is quite unorthodox, but . . . "

"Sir, please move on. I am on duty and unable to converse with civilians."

"But my friend went to school with Dan Hughes, the president's son," Kate said, "and he just wanted you to pass along a message."

"Ma'am, I am unable to—" The agent paused, taking another look at Kate. He appeared to relax just slightly and said, "I'm sorry I interrupted, please go on."

"As I was saying, Bill, here, went to school with the president's son, and when we realized he was here I encouraged him to try and say hello."

Jack said, "I know this sounds odd, but I wrote the president a note, hoping you'd give it to him."

Kate smiled at the agent. "We were hoping if he wasn't too busy he might take five minutes for a quick visit."

Jack jumped in, "I told her there was no way. It was nearly twenty-five years ago. But she talked me into it anyway. If you'd just give him the note, that would be great."

The agent was still looking at Kate when Jack handed him the note. They both thanked the agent profusely and wandered off, window-shopping as they went. The agent had taken the note and put it in his pocket. Now all they could do was wait and hope.

∘ ∘ ∘

The day shift at South Carolina's largest nuclear facility was just ending. Doug Flannery was walking down the hall toward the main chamber when Rick Cortez was exiting, shedding his hardhat and protective eyewear.

"Doug, where you headed? It's time to get a beer."

"Yeah, I know," Flannery told his top supervisor and best friend. "But I've got a strange reading on cylinder four up in the control room, and regulations say I got to check it out."

Cortez laughed. "Doug, you know as well as I do that cylinder four's meter has been on the blink for weeks. What the hell are you thinking?"

"I know, I just have a funny feeling. I don't want a full-scale melt-down on my watch." This time they both laughed. Cortez began to walk away but yelled over his shoulder, "I'll catch you at the Roadkill later."

"You got it," Flannery responded. "But it will probably be late."

Flannery continued his trek to the bowels of the facility, looking down at his clipboard the entire way. His tracking sheet indicated that there was a pressure aberration on cylinder four, but that was not the case today. The pressure readings on #4 had been out of whack for weeks; so another strange reading on the daily log would not have been a surprise to anyone.

As Flannery casually strode through the main chamber, the massive cooling cylinders seemed bigger than ever. His heart was beating at twice the normal rate, and he was gazing from side to side in what he hoped was a casual manner to see if anyone was nearby. When he reached #4, he was completely alone. He took one more look around the massive room and then walked behind the cylinder.

He had practiced this moment in his mind a thousand times in the last twenty-four hours. He quickly took the device that was provided to him out of his infamous fanny pack and placed it right where he knew it would do the most damage. Once the acid in the device melted through the cylinder and into the molten core, a meltdown would occur that would make people forget Three Mile Island. Flannery set the timer on the device and quickly went back to his rounds.

Flannery's rendezvous with his new employers was scheduled for 10:00. He left the facility around 9:45 and drove to the same Motel 6 where they had met previously. As he entered room 112, he had a feeling of déjà vu: Everything looked the same, except that one of the men was not present.

The leader spoke. "Did everything go as planned?"

"Not a hitch," Flannery said, smiling.

The leader gave the woman a slight nod, and she pulled a Nike duffel bag out from under the bed. The leader quickly opened it and showed Flannery the stacks of money he had been promised. It was impossible for him to hide his elation.

At the same moment, the terrorist who was not present in the room was under Doug Flannery's 2003 Ford Taurus. He was disconnecting the ABS sensor and draining the brake fluid into a coffee can. The man quickly finished his job, walked around the corner of the quiet motel, and, as if on cue, the door to room 112 opened. As Flannery drove away from the motel, the lead operative took his cell phone from inside his leather jacket and hit "send." After two rings, someone answered on the other end.

"He's on his way. Synchronize now. And don't be late."

169

o o o

Flannery could not believe his luck. He was driving to his favorite bar $250,000 richer than he had been the previous evening.

As was customary for a director-level employee at the plant, he had set his cruise control at the speed limit to avoid a ticket. Traffic tickets for nuclear engineers were frowned upon nearly as much as they were for pilots. Flannery drove along Highway 119 singing along to the Marshall Tucker Band CD in his player. As he hit his brakes to stop at the 119 and 83 intersection, there was no response.

His immediate reaction was to hit the pedal harder, but the car continued at nearly fifty miles per hour toward the two-way stop. By the time he downshifted to slow the vehicle, it was too late. A speeding eighteen-wheeler smashed into the driver's side of the Ford Taurus, and the consequences were immediate.

o o o

By 6:00 a.m. eastern, the nuclear disaster was reported as the worst in US history. The death of Doug Flannery was merely a page 5 story in the *Columbia Star-Telegram*. By 6:30 a.m., David Ellis was live on CNN, condemning the current administration and reaffirming his support for Senator Hawkins. No one in Vail, other than the president and his staff, was even awake yet.

# thirty-nine

The desk in the corner of the library was lit by two lamps. President Hughes had already read the note twice and was scanning it a third time. When he finally looked up, his face was white as a ghost. "This can't be happening," he stammered.

"I don't believe it," blurted Randy Conner, Hughes's chief of staff. "He's wanted for drug smuggling and attempted murder."

Hughes responded, "We can't ignore his claims. He said more accidents would happen. We have to check this guy out."

"I don't like it," Conner continued. "He's dangerous."

"Not as dangerous as if his accusations are legitimate," replied the president.

"All right, how do you want to handle it?"

"The first meeting is with just you and me. The fewer people who know about this, the better."

"It's only 5:00 a.m. I'll make the call at 7:00," Conner responded.

For the next twenty minutes, the two men went about other Oval Office business. Their discussion of fund-raising down the stretch of the campaign was interrupted by the ringing of Hughes's private line.

He answered with a grunt. For the next thirty seconds, Conner watched the president's expression evolve from anger to fear and finally sadness. He hung up the phone without saying another word.

"That was Sam Wilson," the president said, referring to his secretary of energy. "There's been a nuclear meltdown at a power plant in South Carolina. Not Chernobyl scale, but the worst since Three Mile Island."

It was Randy Conner's turn to go pale. "You're right, this can't be happening." And before he could say another word, the president had lifted the receiver of his private line and begun dialing.

"Who are you calling?" Conner asked.

"Jack McCarthy," Hughes said. "I want to talk to him—now."

o o o

The great room in the Hawkins house in Vail was bigger than the entirety of most New York apartments. The vaulted ceiling was nearly twenty-five feet high, and the river-rock fireplace climbed the entire distance. In one corner was a large pool table, while a full bar adorned the opposite corner. The décor was a mixture of country and Ralph Lauren western. The leather furniture was as soft as butter. A glance out the glass door and across the huge redwood deck revealed a stunning view of Vail Village's Vista Bahn.

Behind the bar, Will Hawkins asked Greg Larson if he wanted anything to drink. Larson declined, wanting to stay sharp, but claiming he'd take one when they were finished.

Will Hawkins was dressed casually but still looked as if he had just stepped out of a magazine ad: handsome, confident, and totally relaxed.

The two men approached the middle of the room. Hawkins planted himself in an oversized leather chair, while Larson took a position on one end of the matching couch. Larson launched into his predetermined line of questioning. His strategy was to lob a series of easy pitches that Hawkins would consistently answer with ease. Once the candidate relaxed, Larson would hit him with a couple of tough ones.

Larson's strategy was working perfectly. Hawkins's well-rehearsed sound bites sounded very presidential, and he was clearly starting to relax. Larson decided it was time to shift gears.

"Tell me how your administration would continue the country's war against drugs," Larson said.

"Our policy will be no tolerance," Will responded. "It is important that we step up our efforts versus where the current administration has been. I believe they're giving lip service to the issue, and our plan is to make a difference."

Larson was smiling inside. It was time to give Hawkins the one-two punch.

"Senator, I know this is a difficult question, but I need to know how you feel about Jack McCarthy, one of your top aides, being implicated in a drug smuggling ring."

For the first time during the interview, Hawkins was speechless. He had more than likely prepared for this type of question, but the easy line of questioning had lulled him out of his usual political defensiveness. Hawkins was quick to recover, however. "It is very disappointing. When I hired Jack from WPC, I expected a significant contribution on our campaign's overall strategic direction, and it was working. So when I first heard the report, I gave Jack the benefit of the doubt and assumed we were dealing with some dirty politics. But as the evidence continues to mount against him, I'm now in the difficult position of having to publicly admit I made a very bad hiring decision. It has been a difficult road. We just hope the public won't be too judgmental surrounding the situation." Hawkins leaned back in his chair, folded his arms, and took in a deep breath. He was obviously happy with the way he handled the answer.

Now for the counterpunch. "Senator, how do you feel about having been the college roommate of the biggest drug trafficker in the free world?"

Hawkins's reaction was priceless. He watched as Hawkins evolved from stunned silence, to fidgety bewilderment, and, ultimately, to overt anger. "I will not dignify that question with a response," the senator blurted.

"But you do want to set the record straight with the American public, don't you? This unfortunate fact must be addressed, don't you think?"

"I thought you were on our side," Hawkins countered.

"I'm not on any side except the side of the truth, and there's clearly some of that needed here."

As the men stared at each other silently, John Rollins crossed the room, explaining that the interview was done for now. But Hawkins waved him off.

"Mr. Larson," Hawkins began, "you do not choose your roommates at Oxford. I also believe it is important to note that neither Carlos Pendrill nor his family were involved in any known illegal activities at the time he and I were roommates. Neither have he and I stayed close since college nor even spoken in more than twenty years. And finally, as a Pulitzer Prize-winning journalist, I can't believe that you don't recognize that this is the type of irrelevant information that has hurt many good, decent men in the past."

"Irrelevant my ass, Senator. This is the type of reporting that helps people choose their next president."

Hawkins took a deep breath and changed his approach.

"Greg, I've had nightmares about this information becoming public. I've considered announcing it myself, but my advisers told me it was political suicide. I cannot go back in time twenty-five years and change the situation, but I would if I could. In my defense, this information does not have an impact on my ability to run this country. So I ask you, as a voting citizen, does having the wrong college roommate make me unfit for office?"

"For me, probably not. But I can't speak for all Americans. My job is to present the facts and let the public decide for themselves."

The room was silent. John Rollins said, "I think that will do it for today. Mr. Larson, I'll arrange for your return trip to Dallas."

# forty

Two men, one dressed in an expensive navy blue suit, the other in the uniform of a US Army general, strolled down the hallway. They were about a hundred feet underground in a top-secret facility code-named Husker. Their conversation was still in the pleasantry stage when they turned left through a vault-like door leading to a viewing area outside a laboratory. The facility resembled a movie set, with scientists behind the thick glass partition executing their tasks, unaware that they were being observed.

Brad Olsen, the director of the facility, was giving Gen. Peter Buffer a tour. "These men and women have made a significant breakthrough in the development of our next chemical weapon. It is a newly developed strain of sarin gas that is harmless in its inert state, but when exposed to a significant force, it becomes the most deadly biological weapon ever invented."

"I'm not sure I understand the benefit," the general asked, seemingly uninterested.

"Well, General, the simplest explanation I can give would be that if I spilled a small amount of the liquid in the laboratory we're now observing, there would be no impact on those people, regardless of whether they were wearing their protective suits or not. However, if I dropped a full test tube of the same liquid from chest-high and it broke on the floor, within ten to twelve seconds of exposure, everyone in that laboratory would die a quick but excruciating death. The beauty of this stuff is our ability to contain the way it spreads. Though it is extremely deadly, it will dissipate in the wind; it will dilute when exposed to water. But used correctly, it will eliminate anyone in the contamination zone. So, while these people's work is still extremely delicate, a small spill that just six months ago would have killed can now be wiped up with a paper towel. And you can obviously envision its usefulness in the type of war we'll be fighting in the future."

The general's reaction was noncommittal.

The two men watched through the glass in interested silence as the scientists continued to work. Just as General Buffer turned to continue his questioning, he was startled by a bright flash from the laboratory. As the two men struggled to comprehend what was happening, they watched the metal shelves holding dozens of sarin test tubes tip toward the floor. Neither man moved as the tubes shattered against one another, spilling clear liquid across the heavily padded floor. The scientists' reactions were equally slow. By the time the group behind the glass consciously realized what had happened, escape was impossible. The inner door had already automatically sealed due to a signal from the floor-level impact sensor. Olsen and Buffer were still paralyzed by disbelief as the scientists fell to the floor, writhing in agony.

As if slapped, the two men looked at each other and at the same instant lurched toward the exit. As they reached the huge metal door, they heard the all-too-familiar clank of the door latching from the outside. They looked at each other, neither able to speak. They were trapped in a tomb; they would never escape.

o o o

Will Hawkins was sitting behind the large mahogany desk in the study of his family's Vail home. As he sat staring out the window at the magnificent view of a steep slope that dropped down into Vail's main village, he pondered his upcoming meeting with Sgt. Maj. Ian McKay. How could things get more fucked up? he wondered to himself. Terrorism, murder, and blackmail. This shit wasn't even believable in Hollywood. But it was happening . . . it was happening to him.

A soft knock at the door startled Will from his thoughts. The door opened, and Ian McKay entered with one of Hawkins's bodyguards.

McKay found himself in awe, entering the lavish office of one of the most powerful men in the free world. He'd been practicing for this moment for months but now found himself speechless. Hawkins gave the bodyguard a nod, and he exited silently.

"Sergeant Major Ian McKay," Hawkins opened formally, "I wish we were meeting under more pleasant circumstances."

"Well, Senator, that makes two of us. You can imagine my discomfort when I discovered that the leading candidate for the world's most powerful office was the man who beat my brother to death in a London alley more than twenty-five years ago." As McKay spoke, he moved toward the massive desk.

Hawkins held up a hand. "Before we go any further, I must inform you that I am armed, so I would suggest you don't try anything silly."

"Senator, I am not here for physical revenge. My revenge is of the monetary sort."

"Well, then, let's get down to business. First, I was completely unaware of the outcome of this unfortunate incident until a few weeks ago. My recollection of the events is vague, but what I do remember is that you and your brother started the fight, and my friend and I ended it in the alley. There is no way we could have known anyone was going to die."

McKay's temper exploded. "You beat him with a piece of wood. You hit him repeatedly, even after he was still. Then you ran. Don't you dare play the innocent! You killed a man, an expectant father of a now beautiful young woman, a woman who never knew her father."

The news struck Hawkins like an electric shock. He had never entertained the idea that McKay's brother was a father. He was completely caught off guard. McKay noticed Hawkins's momentary lapse and seized the opportunity.

"It's never too late to seek redemption, Senator. You can still come forward and admit your role in my brother's death."

Hawkins's face changed in an instant. "Are you fucking crazy?" he screamed. "That happened a long time ago. Do you really believe that I would jeopardize everything I've spent my life working for over a college brawl? Anyway, if I did that, you wouldn't get rich, now would you?"

"First off, the money is not for me. It's for my niece. Secondly, it was not just a college brawl. A man died. My brother died in my arms. His blood is on your hands."

Again, Hawkins was caught by surprise. Hawkins felt he was losing his grip on the situation. He quickly explained why he was willing to meet McKay face to face.

"You know, you truly have balls, Mr. McKay. You walk into the home of the next president of the United States and threaten him for money. Now, until this moment, I had no idea you were doing it for your niece, which makes it all the more difficult to share my news."

"What news is that?"

"Well, to start, I will never be blackmailed. I will not give you one red cent, regardless of the reason. And two, as sorry as I am to say it, you will not be leaving Colorado alive."

As Hawkins spoke, he smoothly leveled a large-caliber handgun at McKay's chest. "I cannot afford for this story to get out. So, this afternoon you will be going hiking in the backcountry. You will become disoriented and ultimately succumb to the elements. We'll try to make it as comfortable as possible, but you will die from exposure. I'm sorry."

As Hawkins finished speaking, two large bodyguards entered the office and wrestled McKay out.

# forty-one

John Rollins and Greg Larson sat across from one another in the spacious study of the Hawkins winter home. The room had thirty-foot-high ceilings with a fireplace that looked to be a replica of the one displayed in the '40s movie *Christmas in Connecticut*. Rollins was doing most of the talking. While the question had yet to be directly asked, Rollins was hoping to ascertain whether Larson would be using the Hawkins/Pendrill relationship as a basis for one of his articles.

Finally, Rollins got around to the question Larson had been waiting for.

"Greg, I have to ask you; what do you plan to do with the information that you have so deftly uncovered?"

"I don't know, John. What do you think I should do?"

"Well, Senator Hawkins is a visionary. His economic and ecological platform is just what this country needs. So I was hoping to not let a college roommate, regardless of his identity, get in the way of that. The future of the US will be a lot brighter with Will Hawkins at the helm."

"You forgot to mention his strong stance on drugs, John. The next president, who professes to be the savior of urban America, was the college roommate of the world's most notorious drug czar. Do you or don't you believe that's news?"

"It's clearly news, Greg," Rollins responded. "The question is whether or not it's relevant."

"Relevant to the broad platforms surrounding the campaign? Probably not. But my fear is that Senator Hawkins is beginning to believe his own bullshit and is going to end up believing he's invincible, that he can get away with anything."

Rollins stared at the floor. The journalist had just put his finger on a worry Rollins had been grappling with for months. But the time to act in that context was behind him; he had worked way too hard to quit now. And the lure of twenty-four hour access to the most powerful man in the world was intoxicating, too close to allow it to slip away.

"Greg, all I can tell you is that Senator Will Hawkins's political career is in your hands. The platform he has set is just what this country needs, and you have to ask yourself: What is more important, the story or our future?"

Larson said nothing.

"Greg, I think the best thing to do is let your conscience be your guide. I've arranged for the Hawkins's other plane to take you back to Dallas this afternoon."

"I appreciate the offer," Greg replied, "but I'm fine catching this afternoon's American flight out of Eagle."

"No need, Greg. It's already set. Someone will meet you downstairs in forty-five minutes."

"John, as much as I appreciate the offer, I'm not taking the senator's plane. I'm already regretting the fact that I rode up with him."

John Rollins stood unsteadily. He was pale and clearly not feeling well.

"Greg, you will be returning to Dallas on the Hawkins jet. If force is necessary, then that can be arranged."

Larson also stood. His reaction was one of confusion. "I'm not sure I understand."

"It's simple, Greg. Senator Hawkins's campaign cannot afford the negative publicity you are suggesting. The Hawkins plane will leave

Eagle airport this afternoon with you on board, and it will explode somewhere over southeastern Colorado."

Larson was completely still, and before he could react, a large man slipped up behind him and, with a single, barehanded blow to the neck, dropped him to the ground, unconscious before he hit.

# forty-two

Jack McCarthy and Kate Anson entered the imposing office of a mountainside mansion in Vail belonging to Paul Anton, one of the wealthiest industrialists in the western United States. Anton was a quiet, reserved billionaire with strong ties to the Republican Party. His Vail vacation home, while understated on the exterior, had one of the most lavish interiors in the entire valley.

Jack and Kate were momentarily stunned. The office was bigger than most apartments and had a view of the Gore Range that took their breath away. The only thing that made their entrance even more memorable was the fact that President Robert Hughes sat behind the exquisite antique desk opposite the doorway. As they stood there motionless, the president stood and waved them to his side of the room.

"Mr. McCarthy, Ms. Anson, I am pleased to make your acquaintance."

"I think I speak for both of us," Jack said, "when I say the feeling is mutual."

With a quick gesture from Hughes, the two Secret Service agents who had escorted Jack and Kate vanished without a word.

"Now that things are a little more intimate, I'm going to get right to the point," Hughes said. "Though the experts on my staff and I don't put a lot of credence in the note you most skillfully passed in my direction,

I think it is fair to say that if there's even the slightest chance that there is any truth in your claims, it would be a mistake on the administration's part not to investigate further. So please, for my own edification, tell me in great detail why one of the wealthiest men in the world, who already has an extremely legitimate shot at the White House, would engage in such madness?"

"Sir," Jack began, "I can't tell you why Senator Hawkins is doing what he's doing, but I can tell you with 100 percent confidence that he is behind this current string of unimaginable disasters."

"What makes you so sure?"

"I overheard him discussing the entire plan. These so-called accidents are not coincidental—nor are they accidents."

Jack went on to recap in great detail everything he had heard that evening outside Hawkins's office. But not even the president, a man with access to all the world's secrets, was prepared for Jack's final statement.

"And, sir, the worst part of this maniacal plan is that his partner is Carlos Pendrill."

The president, known for his quick, nimble mind, was speechless. No one spoke for nearly a minute. Finally, Hughes uttered just two words. "Not possible."

"Mr. President, as much as I'd like to agree, I can't. Not only is it possible, I know for a fact it is true. Will Hawkins and Carlos Pendrill have unleashed a reign of terror on the US with the sole purpose of ensuring that your administration is damaged by the events and that Will Hawkins becomes the next president of the United States."

The president paused for a moment, gathering his thoughts, then grabbed the phone and asked Richard Wright to come to his office immediately. Wright was one of the president's oldest friends and was not only the secretary of state but also the president's most trusted adviser. Wright entered the office just minutes later and was given the abbreviated version of the still unimaginable story. When the briefing was over, his response was very similar to the president's.

"It can't be true. It makes no sense for Will Hawkins to engage in homicidal—shit, genocidal—behavior to get something he has a better than fifty-fifty shot of getting anyway. I don't see the logic. Therefore I have to reject the premise."

The room was again quiet as everyone contemplated what to say next.

Kate spoke first. "Gentlemen, the story Jack has told you is true, yet you refuse to believe him. You've obviously done a background search on Jack and decided he's not a whack job; otherwise, we'd already be locked up. Yet your denials are so vigorous, it's obvious you want to convince us we're mistaken. So what gives? It feels as if you're hiding something."

Richard Wright erupted. "Who the hell do you think you are, accusing the president of the United States of hiding something?"

"Mr. Wright, you know who I am. I'm a trained detective who has spent years gathering evidence as well as observing and participating in verbal gamesmanship. I don't believe you two are giving us the whole story."

"Well, you're wrong!" Wright exclaimed. "The political damage the president is suffering due to these so-called accidents is incalculable."

"If I may," Jack interrupted. "We've gone to great lengths to get here. We've been stalked and shot at; we've stolen cars and inadvertently led another man to his death, all because we believed there was one man in the world who could help us. That's you, Mr. President. But if you won't, then we'll take our chances in going public, because this story must be told. The madness must be stopped. And like it or not, it's the hand Kate and I were dealt. So, are you going to help us or not?"

"Jack," President Hughes said, "as much as I admire your courage and as much as I would like to help, I can't."

At that moment, a hidden side door opened, and in strolled Bo Hawkins. His presence overwhelmed Jack and Kate, and by the time Jack recovered and turned to address the president, Hughes was gone.

"Jack, Kate, you've stumbled on to something much bigger than you can imagine," Wright said. "You see, Will Hawkins actually has been systematically sabotaging President Hughes's campaign via environmental terrorism, which was news to us—and his father, by the way. But now that the plan has been exposed, Mr. Hawkins, here, has come forward with some even more damaging information regarding the president. For that matter, it's information that would be very damaging to the very institution of the presidency and would more than likely have a significant impact on the entire global economy.

"You see, our president is actually a convicted felon. Nearly fifty years ago in a small border town in Texas, a woman of disrepute died while in the company of President Hughes, who at that time was in the drilling business and was being entertained by Mr. Hawkins at the time. He was tried and convicted of negligent homicide in the county court but given a second chance by none other than Mr. Hawkins. He used his connections to gain release for President Hughes and was even able to have the conviction erased from the books.

"Now, you can imagine what information of this type would do to American credibility worldwide, not to mention President Hughes's legacy and personal reputation. So you see, with no hope that this election would proceed according to his wishes without his intervention, Mr. Hawkins has inserted himself into this very awkward situation."

"You've got to be kidding me!" Kate said. "Our president has killed someone, and you're discussing his legacy and reputation and referring to this as awkward? And you, Mr. Hawkins; you're trying to blackmail your son into the White House. All of your asses are mine when we get out of here."

"That's the issue, Ms. Anson," Hawkins said in his slow, Texas drawl. "I can't let you out of here. I've personally accomplished just about everything there is to accomplish in this great land of ours, but being president isn't one of them. Too many skeletons in the closet, if you know what I mean. But my son can become president, and I will die fulfilled. And I'll be damned if the ridiculous antics of a couple of amateur spies are going to get in the way of a real American legacy—the Hawkins legacy. So, as much as I hate to say it, no one who knows you will ever see you alive again. And, to add insult to injury, your clandestine trek here has done a great job of covering your tracks for us. In fact, most people already believe you died in that car explosion down in Denver. Poor bastard."

Hawkins turned and left by the door he had entered. Jack and Kate were ushered out of the office by the Hawkins security team, who had entered as if on cue.

o o o

Greg Larson was shoved into a windowless room in the Hawkins mansion. As the lock clicked behind him, Greg realized he was not alone in the small room. Ian McKay was sitting on a small wooden bench, legs crossed, staring at Greg.

"Who are you?" Greg asked, startled by Ian's presence.

"Sergeant Major Ian McKay, British Special Services."

"I'm Greg Larson. I'm a writer for *The Dallas Free Press*."

The two men shook hands, still trying to comprehend the other's presence.

"Do you mind if I ask what you're doing here?" Greg said.

For the next twenty minutes, Greg and Ian exchanged their backgrounds and the events that had led them to be incarcerated together in the bowels of a house owned by one of America's wealthiest families.

"If we can figure a way out of here, we have enough evidence to decimate one of the world's most powerful families and turn the Democratic party upside down," Greg said.

Ian nodded. "That should have been my plan from the beginning. But I was thinking about my niece. This was, in my mind, some level of compensation for growing up without a father. Now look where I am."

"Let's not focus on how we got into this predicament; let's figure out how we get out of it."

They brainstormed. Finally, they landed on what seemed to be a long shot at best. Ian would fake serious illness. Ian thought he could jab his finger and squeeze out enough blood to give him one significant cough of blood to sell the idea. When the guards intervened to help him to his feet, Ian would try to take them out.

"This plan is so ridiculous, it actually might work," Greg said.

o o o

Jack and Kate had never felt more helpless. "I cannot believe this is fucking happening," Jack said angrily. "We have evidence regarding mass corruption at the highest levels of the US government, and we're locked in a goddamn janitor's closet. We have to find a way out of here."

Kate nodded. "But even if we were to find a way out, we'd immediately be shot as intruders going after the president. The Secret Service does not mess around. The agents who know what's going on will kill to protect the president's reputation, and the ones who don't will kill to protect his life."

Jack thought for a moment. "What if we use the Secret Service to our advantage?"

Kate stared silently.

"Look around. This room is full of equipment that could create or at least simulate a bomb. We could wire me to look like a suicide bomber and at least get the agents to escort us out of the house. After all, they've dedicated their lives to protecting the life of the president at all costs."

"That's creative, Jack, but what about me? There's no reason they would have to take me with you." The tone in her voice seemed to fluctuate between fear and anger.

"Okay, umm . . . You helped me wire the bomb. Now you've decided you don't want to die. You're the demolitions expert who will help them defuse the device."

Kate's shoulders sagged. "This is crazy. Our chances of success are probably in the same range as winning the lottery."

"Do you have a better idea?"

Silence.

"Okay, let's get started. Once they have us outside, we'll just have to take our chances that we can outmaneuver the agents. My guess is only a couple of them will ultimately accompany us to shield the rest of the team from what's really taking place here."

Kate and Jack began scouring the storage room for the appropriate materials.

## forty-three

The office in the Hawkins mansion was silent. Father and son each stared off in separate directions, contemplating the predicament the family legacy had been exposed to. It was obvious that neither wanted to be the first to speak.

Finally, Bo Hawkins broke the silence. "I never liked this plan of yours. I know it's not something you ever considered sharing with me, but I didn't get to where I am by waiting for information to come to me.

"Our current issue is that a small army of people know you're dirty, and that is unacceptable." The longer Bo spoke, the angrier his tone became. "What the hell were you thinking? As a matter of fact, what the hell was I thinking, letting you continue once I understood your intentions?"

Will gave his father a glare of frustration. "Well, it doesn't appear that your little blackmail plan is exactly knocking one out of the park."

"I didn't have a plan, goddammit! My knowledge of the president's past was merely precautionary in case you couldn't win this thing on your own, which clearly you didn't believe you could, based on your actions. Now, before we continue our discussion, don't you ever fucking speak to me in that tone of voice again, because the next time you show me that type of disrespect will be the last time."

The look in his father's eyes made Will look away, trying to hide his fear.

After a brief silence, Bo spoke again. "Now let's finish our little father-son chat. Admittedly, it was a mistake on my part to let your plan continue once I had an idea of what you were contemplating. But I believed if we distanced ourselves from the president and his past, our secrets could remain safe. I also believed that a close race avoided all scrutiny. But now we, or should I say you, are in deep shit, and our only way out is to eliminate our four friends, and stop these damn fool accidents immediately."

Finally Will spoke in nearly a whisper. "There's one more accident planned. But it has the potential to make everyone forget the others."

"It must be stopped!" Bo screamed.

Will's shoulders sagged as he nodded in agreement.

Bo stormed out.

As Will Hawkins sat alone in the spacious office looking out at the grandeur of the Rockies, his thoughts were a thousand miles away. The question of the moment was how to position the ending of the ecoterrorism plot with Carlos Pendrill. There was no simple answer. But the clock was ticking, and the more he thought about it, the more convinced he was that bombing the dam in Washington was a big mistake. Finally, after much internal deliberation, he reached for the phone. After a couple of rings, the familiar gruff reply that signaled Pendrill was bothered by the intrusion resonated on the other end of the line.

"Carlos, Will here."

"What the hell do you want? I thought we were to avoid all contact."

"I've been thinking . . . "

"That's always fucking dangerous."

"We cannot destroy that dam," Hawkins said in a tone that sounded more like a plea than anything else.

Pendrill laughed out loud. "Are you losing your stomach for terrorism, Willie?"

"No, I just believe we've achieved our objective. The damage to the president is done; David Ellis has made sure of that. My inner circle has determined that Hughes is on the ropes. And I believe that any loss of life is no longer necessary."

"Your weakness sickens me, Will. You should have understood your lack of intestinal fortitude before you agreed to the plan."

"Maybe you're right, maybe not. But it doesn't change the fact that I believe we must stop the attack. Can you stop it?"

Pendrill was quiet for a moment. As had been his modus operandi since he was a child, he was trying to turn this situation in his favor.

"I can give it a try, Will. But what's in it for me?"

It was Hawkins's turn to ponder. He knew in his heart that whatever the answer, it was going to cost him dearly. But he also knew there was no choice. So Hawkins stated firmly, "One nonnegotiable request."

Pendrill smiled to himself. This had turned out to be a very rewarding conversation. "I'll see what I can do," were the only words Hawkins heard before the definitive click that ended their conversation.

# forty-four

The small hallway outside the maintenance room was dark and quiet. The two Secret Service agents approached the door confidently. It was lunchtime, and one of them was carrying a tray with a meal that could only be found in the very finest restaurant. The man reaching for the door was thinking, what a waste of good food for a couple of assholes who've got less than twelve hours to live.

As the guards entered the storage room, the first man turned and began preparing a place for the meal tray. The guard carrying the tray noticed Jack first. Sitting on the floor, back against the wall, Jack looked like a high school science project. Wires and duct tape ran all over Jack's chest; taped just under his chin were three sticks of something that looked like dynamite. When the first guard finally turned to see his stunned and unmoving partner, his eyes scanned toward Jack, and he let out a nearly inaudible, "What the fuck?"

"Gentlemen," Jack said, "I think you can quickly identify the grave danger that I represent for your boss, not to mention yourselves."

The lead agent instinctively made a move toward Jack.

"What the fuck are you thinking?" Jack screamed. "You want me to incinerate this entire fucking place before you've even discovered how you can save your boss and your own sorry asses?"

"What do you want?" the second agent asked carefully.

"A dead president or a clean escape. Those appear to be my only options."

The two agents glanced at one another, knowing that neither option was a legitimate choice. But years of training in hostage situations kept them engaging in dialogue.

"Okay, let's discuss this," the lead agent finally said in a calm voice.

"Well, here's how I see it," Jack replied. "I have nothing left. Will Hawkins has taken my life, eradicated any reputation I may have built, and murdered my girlfriend. Killing myself and you crooked fucks doesn't seem like such a bad idea. However, if you two are smart enough to save your own asses, all you have to do is escort us to the nearest forest, walk away, tell your bosses that you did the dirty work, and we all win."

The agents exchanged glances. Obviously, letting the two go was out of the question, but getting the suicide bomber out of the president's residence was the first task. Without a word both agents knew the plan. Do just as McCarthy had asked: Lead the couple to the edge of a nearby remote forest and accelerate the end of their assignment, making it look like a foiled attempt on the president's life.

The first agent finally spoke. "All right, this is against my better judgment, but we'll take you out to the edge of the ski slope and release you. But if you ever fuck us and come out from under the rock where you're hiding, we'll find you and kill you . . . slowly."

"Whatever, man. All I want is to crawl under that rock and forget that I ever got mixed up in your fucked-up world."

The two agents gave Jack and Kate a nod, and the four headed for the mansion's back entrance. Once outside, they began crossing the steep slope. It was apparent to all that anxiety was running high, and the slightest move could ignite the explosive adrenaline that was flowing through all of them.

As planned, once they were far enough away from the house, Kate turned, suddenly screaming, "I don't want to die. Please grab him now before he decides to detonate. He's already told me he doesn't care if he lives or dies."

In response to Kate's sudden movement, both agents had deftly drawn their weapons and were expertly aiming at their respective targets. When they realized what she was saying, they both relaxed slightly. The first agent said, "Jesus, lady, you almost got yourself—"

Kate sent a kick to the nearest agent's groin. As he bent forward in pain, he raised his weapon toward Kate. Before he could aim, Kate kicked him on the side of his neck with perfect accuracy, rendering him immediately unconscious. At the same instant, Jack delivered a side-hand blow to the second agent's neck but without the same result. The agent bulled into Jack like an NFL linebacker, tackling him to the ground.

The next fifteen seconds were some of the most brutal Kate had ever seen. Both men were trained to fight, and both also knew they were fighting for their lives. Kate felt helpless but watched intensely, waiting for a moment where she could actually help Jack.

The second agent had gained the advantage and was repeatedly driving his fist toward Jack's face. However, his neck was completely exposed, so Kate threw her entire weight into a chop. He immediately went limp and fell over.

Jack and Kate looked at each other and quickly ducked into the woods to regroup. Blood was streaming from Jack's nose, but all his body parts appeared to be in working order. He quickly stripped off his "bomb," and they ran down the slope toward Vail.

# forty-five

The incessant banging from inside the locked room had taken its toll on the two bodyguards in the hallway outside. Finally, the bigger of the two gargantuan men said, "Fuck it," and rose from his chair to see what all the noise was about.

"What are you doing?" asked the second guard. "Our orders were extremely clear: Under no circumstances are we to enter that room."

"Yeah, yeah. But I can't take this banging anymore. Anyway, these guys can't take us. Let's see what's up."

Greg Larson was still pounding on the reinforced door when he heard the deadbolt click. As he stepped away, the two massive guards filled the doorway.

"What is going on here?" the first guard asked.

Greg pointed to Ian McKay, writhing on the floor. His convulsions were so severe he appeared to be having an epileptic fit.

"What's wrong with him?" the second guard asked.

"How the fuck do I know? I've been trying to get you assholes to help for the last twenty minutes."

Ian rose to his hands and knees, choked violently, and coughed up a large glob of blood.

"Jesus!" the second guard exclaimed. "What should we do?"

"Get him some medical help, dumbass," Greg said.

McKay dramatically collapsed back to the floor; his chest wasn't moving. The two guards stared for a few seconds, then one of them leaned down to get a closer look.

"Shit, man, I think he's dead," he said to his partner. "Let's get him outta here."

As they lifted the limp and unresponsive McKay, they struggled to stand. Just as they got him to a standing position, he slipped awkwardly. The two guards struggled to keep their balance, and that's when McKay struck. In less than five seconds, both guards were immobilized.

"Jesus!" Greg exclaimed. "How did you do that?"

"It's actually quite simple," McKay responded. "I'll teach you someday. But we need to get out of here. They'll only be like that for a couple of minutes."

Ian quickly searched the guards' pockets, looking for anything useful. When he pulled out a set of car keys for a Chevy Suburban, he turned to Greg and said, "These should come in handy."

The two men walked down the long basement hall, searching for the stairs that would lead them to the garage. As they approached the stairs, they heard two men enter the house, deep in conversation. Ian and Greg froze, and the voices began to fade as the unseen men went toward the kitchen of the Hawkins mansion.

Greg and Ian quietly ascended to the large mudroom just inside the garage. They listened to make sure no one was on the other side of the door. When they were sure it was clear, they quietly slipped into the spacious four-car garage. Only two vehicles were inside. Ian studied the keys and quickly determined which "Texas Cadillac" belonged to them. He tossed the keys to Greg and gestured with his head toward the one on the left as he opened the driver's door of the other vehicle and popped the hood. Ian reached in toward the engine, grabbed a handful of wires, and ripped them from the vehicle. He quickly jumped in on the passenger side of the black Suburban, looked at Greg, and reached for the garage door remote.

As the garage door opened slowly, a startled Hawkins bodyguard inside the house ran to see what was going on. When he opened the door to the garage, he saw Ian and Greg sitting in the Suburban with the engine running. He quickly reached for the garage door button on the wall and reversed the progress of the door. Greg realized what was happening, slammed the truck into reverse, and crashed through the descending panel door.

Greg and Ian were out and racing down the small, winding Vail Village road. They were almost to the first intersection when a man and woman darted out from behind a cluster of pine trees and waved wildly for the vehicle to stop. Greg's inclination was to continue driving until he realized that the man flailing his arms by the side of the road was someone he'd come to recognize in the newspaper headlines.

Greg slammed on the brakes, and Jack McCarthy and Kate Anson jumped into the vehicle. Greg wasn't sure what made him decide to blindly pick up these fugitives, but it had been a very strange forty-eight hours. Once the vehicle was rolling again, the four hurriedly compared notes. They quickly realized that their best chance for survival was to reach the relative anonymity of Denver.

The race was on.

# forty-six

The stolen Suburban was barely on I-70 heading east to Denver when Greg Larson exclaimed, "Run that by me again? You went to the president of the United States to warn him of Hawkins's psychotic plan, only to find out his daddy owns the presidency as well? This cannot be fucking happening!"

"It is," Jack said. "And we're the only ones who can stop that arrogant prick from waltzing straight into the White House."

"Agree," Ian said, "but let's make sure we know exactly what we're doing when we get to Denver. Any mistake could be our last."

They began discussing their options for contacting authorities, while at all times protecting the evidence: themselves.

"Oh, shit," Greg said, his eyes flickering from the road ahead to the rearview mirror. "There's a car in the left lane, closing fast."

As the speeding SUV began to pass the stolen Suburban, the four gave a collective sigh of relief. But just then, the Ford Expedition swerved to the right and clipped the left front fender of the Suburban, forcing it to lurch to the right, off the steep embankment of Vail Pass. Greg was able to keep the large truck from rolling, but in order to do that, he had the vehicle hurtling down the steep incline, nose first. All four occupants were screaming, not even knowing they were doing it.

Much to their surprise, the truck neither rolled nor slammed into the rapidly approaching trees but instead rolled to a graceful stop in the drainage swale at the edge of the large forest.

The moment the vehicle came to rest, Ian McKay screamed, "Everyone out! We've got to get to the forest before those guys get down the embankment!"

All four fugitives jumped from the SUV. Kate screamed, "Shit! Something cut my leg."

Ian leaned down to get a closer look and saw a lot of blood. Worse yet, some sort of metal object was stuck in Kate's leg. While Ian was inspecting more closely, a strange pop could be heard from up the hill, and within a second, the night sky was illuminated by a phosphorescent flare. The group was completely exposed on the valley floor, and shots rang out almost immediately.

They all scrambled behind the black Suburban and waited. When the flare faded, Ian again took charge and ordered the group to sprint toward the refuge of the large forest. As they sprinted the twenty-some-odd yards toward safety, another flare lit up the sky. As the group watched their pursuers scanning the valley floor from above, they realized they had not seen them make it into the forest.

As Ian tended to Kate's wound, Jack asked, "What now?"

"Ms. Anson will not be able to make it far. Her wound is very serious, and she's lost a good amount of blood. You two should leave now. I'll wait with her and take care of our friends when they come down for a closer look."

"I'm not leaving!" Jack said. "Kate and I have been through too much to not finish this thing together."

"Jack, don't be an ass," Kate said sternly. "This is no time to be gallant. We have to nail these bastards, and if splitting up increases our odds, then let's get on with it."

Jack stared at her a moment, then nodded without saying another word and pushed deeper into the forest with Greg Larson right behind him.

The two men who had run the Suburban off I-70 were cautiously making their way down the steep embankment. Each man was angling away from the other in an effort to cover more ground. As they continued their descent, Ian watched closely from the edge of the woods, obscured by some thick brush. Not only was he intently making sure he didn't lose sight of either man, but he was also scanning his immediate surroundings, trying to formulate a plan.

Ian had hidden Kate nearby in a small creek bed, covering her with small tree limbs and brush. The two pursuers were nearly at the bottom of the hill when Ian made his decision. As the pursuers continued to put distance between themselves, Ian would move to his left and patiently wait behind a small rock outcropping. When the first pursuer got close enough, he would immobilize him and take his automatic weapon. What was paramount in this process was to ensure the entire search took long enough for Jack and Greg to get a major head start, in case he was unsuccessful in his attempt to eliminate the guards. At the same time, Ian also felt compelled to stay close to Kate in case she was discovered.

After moments of quiet tension, the man who had circled to Ian's left was getting increasingly close to the rock sanctuary. Ian slowly reached for a stone. When the stalker was less than twenty feet away, Ian threw the golf-ball-sized rock over his left shoulder. The man stopped, assessed where he thought the noise had come from, and picked up the pace toward his prey.

As the man passed the outcropping of rocks, Ian thought to himself that it almost seemed too easy. He quickly stuck his left foot out just as the man was passing. In one swift move, he grabbed the barrel of the gun with his left hand while wrapping his right arm around the neck of his pursuer. As the man fell toward the ground, his own inertia, coupled with precision positioning of Ian's right arm, broke his neck instantly. Ian caught the dead man and lowered him to the ground silently. But when the full weight of the dead man came to rest, a small rock pushed into the communication device that was placed on his belt, sending a loud series of beeps off into the quiet of the forest.

The second man stopped in his tracks and called out for his partner. Nothing but silence answered. The suspicion accompanying the silence caused the man to back off slightly and stare directly toward Ian's safe haven.

Ian was stuck. Any movement could cause the second pursuer to fire in his direction, knowing that he hadn't heard from his partner. Then, as luck would have it, a small animal moved off to the second man's left, diverting his attention for a few seconds. The diversion allowed Ian to quickly distance himself from the corpse.

It was again time to wait. Ian was well positioned behind a huge lodgepole pine, waiting for President Hughes's henchman to come his way. After what seemed like an eternity, the man was nearly there. Once he passed, Ian lunged toward him and delivered a heavy blow to the side of his neck. The man staggered as if he were going to fall but then turned, smiling, his weapon aimed directly at Ian's midsection.

Ian was stunned. The man said, "Not turning out the way you planned? Now I need you to lead me . . ." But before he could finish, he dropped to his knees and collapsed, blood running down below his ear. Much to Ian's surprise, directly in front of him was Kate, holding a large rock and weakly smiling. Then she, too, fell to the ground in a bundle.

# forty-seven

Jack and Greg had been hiking for hours. While the pitch had never been too steep, it had been a consistent uphill climb, and both men were exhausted. The faint light in the sky told them that dawn was approaching, and though the fall night air was quiet and cool, the strenuous climb had both men perspiring.

"Thank God we found that logging road," Jack panted. "We would have been hopelessly lost if we'd had to hike through the forest the entire way."

Both men were breathing hard when Greg stopped in his tracks to listen. A faint sound was whispering through the predawn air. As the noise grew louder, both men looked at each other, realizing there was some sort of vehicle approaching. It didn't sound like a car, but it was clearly mechanical. As the sound grew louder, the two men scurried off the logging road, not sure what they would encounter. Then over the rise came a man riding a large all-terrain vehicle. He was clearly alone. Both men rose to their feet and walked to the center of the road to flag down the rider.

Surprised by the presence of two men clearly not prepared to spend the night out in the Colorado mountains, the rider came to an abrupt halt. As he removed his helmet, he asked, "What the hell are you guys doing out here?"

Jack and Greg exchanged glances and realized they hadn't actually thought about what their answer to a question like that might be.

"Well," Jack stammered, "our car was run off the road last night, and rather than climb back up the steep pitch to the highway, we thought we could find an easier way back to the road. Then we found this logging road and . . . well, we're fucking hopelessly lost. What are you doing out here?"

The man smiled and answered, "I work for a snowmobile touring operation, and I'm headed up to our base camp to begin preparing it for winter." The men stood there not knowing what to say next when the rider said, "You guys could probably use something to eat and drink."

Jack and Greg immediately perked up, not realizing just how depleted they were. The rider took out two bottles of water and a couple of energy bars, and the two men quickly downed the food and water without saying another word. When they were finished, the rider told the two men to get in the small bed of the Ranger ATV so he could take them to the top of Vail Pass where they could call the authorities.

At the mention of calling the police, Jack and Greg exchanged glances. As the rider turned the vehicle around, the two men's minds raced. Over the next ten minutes, as the ATV bumped along the rutted, washed-out dirt road, each man contemplated individually how to ditch this good Samaritan gracefully and continue their trek to Denver.

The Rocky Mountain sky was lightening by the minute as the bumpy ride back to civilization continued. Then without any warning to Greg, Jack tapped the rider on the shoulder and yelled, "Do you mind if we stop for a second so I can take a leak?" The rider obliged without thinking twice. When Jack was done, he returned to the vehicle and stated, "I know this is going to seem odd, but we are not in a position to contact the authorities at this time, and we're going to need to borrow your vehicle for a while."

"The fuck you are," the rider responded and quickly reached for the ignition.

Jack grabbed the man's arm. "Look, this is not what it seems, and we have no desire to hurt you, but we're desperate men. We have to get to

Denver immediately, and you just happened to be in the wrong place at the wrong time. Now, please get off the vehicle, and we'll make this as painless as possible."

The rider did as he was told, but once off the vehicle he lunged for Jack, hoping to catch him by surprise. The response was quick and effective.

Greg looked stunned.

"I told you I was a black belt, didn't I?" Jack said with a smile. "He'll be fine, other than a pretty wicked headache when he wakes up."

Then Jack reached down, found the keys to a Ford F-150 in the man's front pocket, and said, "Let's get him in the back of the ATV and find that truck so we can get to Denver."

A few minutes later, the men were pulling into the rest stop at the top of Vail Pass with the orange dawn sky greeting them. There were only two vehicles in the parking lot: a Ford F-150 and another pickup truck with a camper shell on the back. Jack pulled the four-wheeler right up to the back of the camper and jumped out. He knocked quietly on the rear door and waited. When no one responded, Jack looked all over the parking lot to ensure that no one was watching. Then, more easily than Greg thought possible, he broke the small window above the doorknob, reached in, and unlocked the door. The two men quickly loaded the unconscious rider in the back of the camper, ditched the ATV in a nearby ravine, and hopped into the Ford pickup.

"By the time he comes to and finds a phone or flags someone down," Jack said, "we should be in Denver."

As the men pulled out of the parking lot, another ATV, obscured by a hill, was pulling into the parking lot, headed straight toward the camper. The man and woman on the ATV didn't notice the Ford F-150 leaving the parking lot. The two riders hadn't gone very far when they decided it was still too cold to go off-roading and that their best bet was to return to the camper and keep each other warm until later in the morning. As the two, very enthralled with each other, neared the pop-up camper on the back of an older Dodge pickup, they simultaneously realized something was wrong.

With the small back window above the camper doorknob smashed, it was apparent their truck had been broken into. What they weren't prepared for was the unconscious man lying on the pickup bed. When the young man cautiously opened the camper door, his girlfriend let out an involuntary scream that made him jump twelve inches in the air. "Jesus, Kelly, you scared the shit out of me," he exclaimed.

"I couldn't help it. Is he dead?"

"I don't think so," he replied as the man groaned and rolled to his side on the camper floor.

Without a word, the two ran to the front of the truck and hopped in the cab, fighting to get their hands on their cell phones. Within twenty minutes, the Colorado Highway Patrol had arrived at the deserted rest area.

# forty-eight

Two of President Hughes's most trusted men sat at the kitchen table of a small condominium just off Interstate 70 in Silverthorne. Both of them were drinking Diet Pepsis, staring at the police radio on the table in front of them. They had been monitoring the Colorado Highway Patrol frequency for the past ninety minutes, hoping to get a break on the search for Jack McCarthy and Kate Anson.

Both men were growing weary and agitated. Where had McCarthy and Anson gone? Just when one of the men rose to stretch, an APB was issued to all on-duty highway patrolmen: A vehicle had been hijacked from a workman on the top of Vail Pass just thirty minutes ago. Make: Ford F-150. Color: white. License plate: Colorado 681-DNT.

"Bingo!" one of them yelled as they raced toward the door. Both men were in the parking lot in seconds, jumping into their silver Jeep Grand Cherokee, heading toward I-70.

"Which way do you think they headed?" the man riding shotgun asked the driver.

"I've got to believe they're heading toward Denver. That's going to be the easiest place for them to get lost and regroup. But to be safe, let's alert our sentries monitoring both directions, and we'll head east toward Denver."

The next five minutes were filled with multiple scrambled cell phone calls to various lookouts, instructing them to watch for the stolen Ford truck. Both men now believed that the two most likely contact points would be the sentries on the east side of the Continental Divide and those at the small tourist town of Georgetown.

As the Jeep approached the west side of the 1.7-mile Eisenhower Tunnel, none of the alerted sentries had spotted anything. Then, a caller from the other side of the tunnel spotted the white Ford. The passenger in the Jeep was issuing the instructions to follow the truck, maintain visual contact, and wait for them to catch up, when he suddenly screamed, "Shit!"

"What?" said the driver, twisting his head to look at his partner.

"We lost the cell in the tunnel."

"No worries, we'll catch them in less than five minutes." He pressed on the accelerator.

o o o

Jack and Greg were discussing their plan for when they reached Denver. Greg's roommate from the University of Missouri, Scott Holly, was a well-known columnist at *The Denver Morning News*. The plan was to reach the downtown offices of the newspaper and contact Scott. With a little luck, they could secure a private office and begin their work. First, they would get video documentation of Jack detailing his experience with the Will Hawkins campaign. Simultaneously, Greg would begin a series of articles outlining the criminal activities associated with both the current administration and the Democratic front-runner. No one at the *News*, beyond Scott, could be trusted, Greg said.

The stolen Ford F-150 was only a few miles from the small, rundown mining town of Silver Plume when Jack noticed a Jeep Cherokee behind them that had been there much too long. Jack slowed the truck to see if the Jeep would pass. When it did not, Jack stated very matter-of-factly, "I think we have company."

Greg quickly turned to check the vehicle, telegraphing to the pursuers that they had been spotted. The driver of the Jeep jammed the accelerator to the floor just as Jack did the same. Both vehicles accelerated, hurtling down the 6 percent grade, passing the runaway truck ramps prominently featured on the steep slope. The Jeep was gaining on the pickup as both vehicles approached eighty miles per hour. They reached a straightaway, and the passenger in the Jeep leaned out of his window and aimed at the Ford with his government-issue .44 magnum. The slug shattered the back window.

"Son of a bitch!" Greg yelled, ducking as low as he could.

Jack said, "Climb into the back and see if there's anything you can throw at them to slow them down."

Greg looked at Jack and burst out laughing.

"You have any better ideas?" Jack yelled as he veered across both lanes, trying to throw off the gunman's aim. Greg clambered into the back seat of the extended cab and, as the truck swerved wildly, started digging through the tools piled on the seat and the floor between the seats. As he was deciding on his first weapon, a shot hit him in the left shoulder, knocking him to the floor in the back seat.

Greg dragged himself back up on the seat and inspected his shoulder. It appeared the bullet had passed through the fleshy part of the upper arm, missing both bone and tendon. While there was a significant amount of blood and it hurt like hell, Greg was still reasonably functional. Adrenaline was pumping through his veins, and now he was pissed.

Another bullet whizzed through the cab of the truck as Greg launched a small sledgehammer out the window; it landed harmlessly in front of the pursuing Jeep. Next he flung a large file, also missing the mark. Finally, with all the strength he could muster, he threw a large clawhammer, and it connected with the pursuing vehicle. It smashed into the driver's side windshield and shattered the safety glass, and the Jeep swerved sharply. Next he threw a crescent wrench, which also hit the speeding vehicle. The gunman, for the moment, retreated to the safety of the vehicle's interior.

Jack knew that the reprieve would not last long. Traveling at close to ninety miles per hour, he decided to gamble that the pursuers were not as familiar with this stretch of the interstate as he was. About one and a half miles before the small mountain community of Georgetown, there was an exit to a scenic overlook parking lot where tourists could view a trestle bridge spanning Clear Creek on the historic Georgetown Narrow Gauge Railway.

Jack approached the exit to the overlook without slowing. Then without warning, he locked up the brakes on the pickup and swerved to the right into the small parking area. The silver Jeep followed, barely missing the guardrail on the far side of the entrance. Jack accelerated through the tiny lot, swerving hard left to re-enter I-70 on the other side. The driver of the Jeep was still correcting from his narrow miss at the entrance when he saw Jack swerve left. His instinct was to do the same. However, the vehicle was not in position to make an opposite turn that severe, and the Jeep began to roll. As Greg crawled up off the seat following Jack's bizarre series of stunts, he saw the Jeep roll over the edge of the overlook, disappearing toward the creek and rocks in the canyon below.

"Slow down," he yelled. "We lost them; or more accurately, they lost it."

Jack glanced into the back seat. "We need to stop and fix your shoulder."

"I'll worry about the shoulder; you get us to Denver."

# forty-nine

The fifty-five-minute drive from just outside George-town to Denver went quietly and smoothly. Though both Jack and Greg were convinced that another brush with the law was highly likely, they ultimately decided that finding another vehicle along the reason-ably uninhabited stretch of I-70 was probably more dangerous. There were three separate incidents where Jack was sure they were spotted, but pure luck or divine intervention allowed them safe passage to the relative obscurity of the big city.

The offices of *The Denver Morning News* were located on Colfax Avenue, just blocks from the state's capitol. Jack found a covered park-ing garage nearby and pulled into a space on the second floor, where they abandoned the now-trashed Ford pickup. Greg found a well-worn pea coat in the backseat of the truck and did his best to put it on. With the damaged shoulder and bloodstained shirt as well hidden as possible, the two men made the short trek toward the newspaper's headquarters. As they entered the main lobby, Jack trailed a half step behind Greg, ready to catch him if he stumbled or lost consciousness. Greg, clearly running on adrenaline, straightened up as he approached the security guard behind the reception desk. "We're here to see Scott Holly."

The guard laughed out loud. "It's not even 9:00," the guard said, continuing to chuckle. "It's rare for Mr. Holly to be here anytime before 10:00."

"Give it a try, will you?" Greg responded. "Scott and I were college roommates, and I was hoping to surprise him before I have to head out to the airport."

The guard shrugged. "Name?"

"Can't we make it a surprise?" Greg pleaded innocently.

The guard dialed. He waited a moment, then his eyes widened when the phone was answered. "Mr. Holly," he said, "it's Phil, down in front. I've got a visitor here for you . . . No, he says he's a friend, here to surprise you. All right, then. Thanks."

The guard looked up at Greg, "He said he'll be right down."

When the elevator doors opened, Scott Holly immediately spotted Greg across the lobby. "Larson!" he yelled. "What the hell are you doing here?"

As he strode across the lobby, he realized something was up.

"Jesus, man, what happened to you?"

Then he looked over and saw Jack. "Hey, that's the guy—"

Greg interrupted, "Can we finish this conversation upstairs?"

"Sure," Scott responded quietly.

The three men rode the elevator to the seventh floor in silence. Finally, Greg looked over at Scott and said, "Scott Holly, Jack McCarthy." The two men shook hands. "Scott, we need a conference room for the day. And it would be great if you didn't let anyone know we were here."

"What the hell is going on, Greg?"

"I'll tell you when we get in the conference room."

Five minutes later, the three men were in a conference room with the blinds pulled. Greg and Jack alternated telling their story to Scott. His jaw hung in disbelief as they relayed the entire saga.

When they were finished, Greg looked at Scott and said, "I can assure you this is not a prank. This is the story of the last hundred years."

"What do you need from me?" Scott finally responded.

"A laptop, a video camera, and a discreet doctor," Greg said, revealing his shoulder for the first time.

"The computer and the camera should be easy. But Jesus, Greg, it looks like you should go to the hospital."

"Not yet, man. But once we're ready to contact the FBI, I'm sure I'll get plenty of top-notch medical treatment."

Scott hesitated, then said, "I'll see what I can do." He turned toward the door.

"Scott," Greg called. Scott turned back toward him. "No one but the doctor, please."

"Got it," he said as he left the two men alone in the small, cluttered room.

"I've got to call my boss," Greg said.

"No, it's too soon," Jack responded. "It's a long time until tomorrow's edition of *The Dallas Free Press* hits the streets."

"Jack, Tom Johnson is the editor of the nation's seventh-largest newspaper. He's built his career on the ability to maintain confidentiality and protect his sources. He can be trusted. Plus, I need him to reserve space for my first installment of the story that's going to rock the world."

Jack was quiet for a while. "All right, you can call. But don't tell him where we are yet."

"Deal," Greg responded, reaching for the phone.

Tom Johnson was in his office, and after a brief tirade directed at Greg for not keeping in touch, he remained quiet as Greg relayed the entire story. When Greg finished, there was silence on the other end of the line.

"Tom?" Greg said.

"Jesus, Larson, are you crazy? You expect *The Dallas Free Press* to run a story that accuses the president of the United States and one of the most powerful families in the world of murder, conspiracy, ecoterrorism, and just about every other felonious crime I can think of? Not going to happen."

"Tom, this is about truth. It's about justice. And I would venture to say, it's about a guaranteed Pulitzer."

Johnson sighed on the other end of the line. "Can we prove it?"

"Absolutely," Greg said excitedly. "I've got Jack McCarthy right here. We're going to record his testimony. I'll write the first article of the series. We'll contact the FBI. And then we have to find Ian McKay and Kate Anson before the bad guys do."

Johnson responded, "That reminds me, a guy with a British accent left a message on my voicemail saying he had some information for your story."

"Anything else?" Greg said.

"Yeah, he left his cell number," Johnson responded, reading the number into the receiver.

"Tom, save me the space, and I'll be in touch."

o o o

When the line went dead, the man sitting in the service van parked on Commerce Street outside of the *Free Press* building thought to himself how predictable people were. He had guessed it was only a matter of time before Larson would contact his boss at the paper. What was next was also on his mind: Six outsiders now knew the truth. Five would soon be reunited in Denver at *The Denver Morning News* or some other location according to his tracing equipment. The sixth was right upstairs. Two quickly assembled jobs could clean up this entire mess.

But something was nagging at him: It was Will Hawkins who was in deep shit, not him. Not to mention that setting up two jobs in the next few hours was not going to be a simple process. Then in an instant, he knew what to do next. He crawled from the console in the back of his van into the driver's seat and slowly drove away. Fuck it, he thought. Camelot for the next millennium would soon be officially finished.

Hours later, Jack McCarthy finished recording his incredible story. As he hit eject, Marc Hoffman, the local FBI chief, reached for the disk. Almost simultaneously, Greg hit send on his borrowed laptop, and his first story in a series was electronically sent to Tom Johnson at *The Dallas Free Press*. The FBI had graciously agreed to keep a lid on the story so that the world would get this news the old-fashioned way, via the newspaper. Jack and Greg looked worn but relieved. The two men shook hands and followed the FBI agents to the vehicle that would take them to a safe house. Medical treatment was awaiting Greg. When they reached the safe house, Ian and Kate were already there.

# fifty

Pendrill's elite group of terrorists had been completely isolated from any news associated with the phenomenon that the media had dubbed "Terrogate." While the entire US political system was being scrutinized from top to bottom, the four Mexican nationals were holed up in a small town in Washington, planning their final act of ecoterrorism.

As the foursome approached the guard shack at the Columbia River hydroelectric facility, each member of the team was keenly aware of his or her specific assignment. The woman was made up to appear as if her car had rolled off an embankment, and her injuries had left her wandering aimlessly in the desolate area. The team leader had veered off to the left to hide behind a large boulder and wait for an opportunity to take out the guard. The other two men hung back, waiting for Phase I of the plan to be executed.

As the woman got closer to the shack, it became apparent that there was no one manning the station. The woman broke into a huge grin and waved the others toward the first rendezvous spot. As the four gathered, clearly pleased with the absolute lack of security, the leader smiled and stated in perfect English, "This may be our easiest target yet."

The target was the dam itself. With some strategically placed extreme-temperature explosives, the dam would produce easily detectable cracks on its exterior, warning the world hours or days before the structure would actually give way. The subsequent collapse would send a hundred-foot wall of water barreling down the now-uninhabited narrow canyon as hundreds of news cameras from around the world chronicled the event. It was the terrorists' grand finale before returning to Mexico to collect their bounty.

The four terrorists approached the massive steel door that was the entrance into the facility. There was still no sign of any security or maintenance personnel. The woman held a penlight for the leader as he pulled a sophisticated toolkit from his backpack. He immediately went to work on the industrial lock. Less than two minutes later, a distinct clicking sound indicated they had gained access to the power plant.

The four terrorists moved swiftly down the narrow passages toward the center of the facility where they were to place the explosive charges. The leader raised his right fist to halt the group. They all listened for any indication that their presence had been detected. Everything was quiet except for the pounding of their own hearts, which sounded like a jackhammer to each of them individually. The leader consulted the blueprints that indicated their destination was less than thirty meters away, around the next corner. He signaled for them to move slowly toward the dam's epicenter. The terrorists proceeded cautiously to their destination.

As they reached the core of the dam, a floodlight illuminated a small unit of elite US Marines, all with automatic weapons aimed at one of the four terrorists. The reflex was the same for each of them; they spun on their heels ready to retreat but were met by a second marine squad, weapons trained.

A voice on a bullhorn commanded, "Please drop your weapons, raise your hands, and back slowly up against the wall." All of the terrorists were seemingly complying when two of them swung their automatic weapons toward the second set of marines. Before the second terrorist had even fired a shot, both marine units selectively opened fire. The ensuing firefight lasted less than five seconds. When the shots ceased, all four terrorists were dead.

# epilogue

Jack McCarthy sat alone on the balcony of his recently purchased Vail penthouse. It had been just over twelve months since he and Kate had escaped from the Hawkins family's slope-side mansion, and the autumn air sent chills of memories down his spine. As Jack gazed up at North America's premier ski destination, he couldn't stop thinking about Kate.

After the story broke, Jack and Kate had returned to Dallas. The media frenzy surrounding their arrival was comparable to that surrounding the Kennedy assassination in 1963. Endless questions and interview requests, most of which were denied, began taking their toll on both of them. This, coupled with Jack's guilt surrounding Carrie's violent death, forced him into isolation.

He told everyone, including Kate, he just needed to sort some things out. By the time he had, it was too late: Kate, devastated by his callousness, withdrew from him.

Jack sat in the crisp mountain air and pondered all that had happened. Bo and Will Hawkins had been indicted for murder and conspiracy to commit murder, along with a host of other charges, and were currently awaiting trial. Jack's testimony was complete; he had chosen to submit it electronically to avoid the media rigors of the trial. President

Hughes resigned before impeachment proceedings could get underway. The speculation in the media was that he had traded his testimony against the Hawkins men for what was left of his freedom. Richard Willis, Hughes's vice president, easily won the Republican nomination but was soundly defeated in the general election by Ray Langston, the US Representative from Oregon. After winning one of the most closely chronicled elections in world history, Langston named David Ellis, leader of The Future State Foundation, as his secretary of the interior.

And, finally, Carlos Pendrill was apparently in hiding somewhere in central Mexico, evading the extradition ruling that would put him on trial in the US for masterminding the series of devastating environmental catastrophes.

Jack hoped that the American public was sufficiently sickened by the shocking revelations surrounding this tragic episode in our country's history and would demand an end to the big-money candidates and their vicious campaigns that focused on discrediting the competitor versus communicating a candidate's platforms and values. And, in fact, campaign reform legislation was already in process on the Hill, focusing not only on financial reform but also on message ethics in an effort to restore credibility to the US political system.

Jack had declined the offer to rejoin WPC, the agency where he had achieved such success. The haunting memories of a simpler time and the loss of a woman he had loved precluded him from ever even considering a return.

Ian McKay had returned to England. The ransom he had sought for his niece had materialized from a very unlikely source, Esther Hawkins, Will's mother, had gladly given the money to Ian. She was so disgraced by the actions of her husband and son that she had spent the last year donating the Hawkins family fortune to any worthy cause she could find.

Kate Anson had returned to work on the Dallas police force. After months of constant ribbing from the guys at the station, her work life had gotten somewhat back to normal.

Jack's next career was looking to be much more lucrative—and tumultuous. He had just signed a book deal with a major publisher to chronicle the entire incident. The $10 million advance he had received was the largest in publishing history, and it afforded Jack his luxurious new digs. His three compadres had rebuffed his offer to share the wealth; Greg Larson had already signed his own book deal, Ian McKay had declined on principle . . . and Kate had simply not responded.

As he looked up at the ski slope across the valley, he couldn't help thinking that he was living a dream that was funded by a nightmare. He was semiretired, writing a book, and living in a slope-side penthouse, yet all he felt was emptiness.

He thought about Kate constantly. He was embarrassed by how he had treated her, and she had not responded to any of his overtures. He knew in his heart that he needed her, but he also knew that it was time to move on.

Jack glanced at his watch and realized Ian McKay would be arriving soon. While Ian had declined any of the proceeds surrounding the unsavory events of the past year, he did agree to an annual, all-expense-paid trip to Vail to visit with his new friend. Jack heard a car door slam outside, but when the doorbell rang, it still startled him; he hadn't had many visitors recently. Jack opened the door and greeted Ian with a handshake and a hug.

"It's good to see you, Ian. Where are your bags?"

"Down in the car," Ian said, an odd smile playing across his face.

"Well, let's get them so we can go have a beer."

As the two men walked down the outdoor corridor, they chatted about Ian's trip to the States. They stood side by side, waiting for the elevator that would transport them to the ground floor. When the elevator door opened, Jack was stunned. Standing in front of him was the one person he'd never expected to see. Kate Anson was more beautiful than he had remembered. For what seemed like an eternity, neither of them spoke or made a movement. Then, simultaneously, they reached for each other and embraced. No one said a word, but all of them knew Jack and Kate needed each other. Then Jack smiled and took Kate's hand, and the three of them headed back toward the penthouse that suddenly, Jack realized, felt like a home.

# about the author

Mike Sweeney graduated with a degree in journalism from Colorado State University, where he developed a strong passion for advertising. He began his career in the ad industry in Dallas, later moving to Los Angeles before returning to his roots in Colorado. Spending a significant amount of time on planes over the years allowed him to complete this novel, written because he always said he would and finished with the support of many. Mike is the chief executive officer of The Integer Group. A native Coloradan, he currently splits his time between Evergreen and Chicago. Mike lives with his wife of nearly twenty-five years, Pat, and is father to Jack; stepfather to Janci and Spencer; Poppa to Madison, Pearl, Lucian, and Clara; and a friend and colleague to many.